BLOOD MOON

Jeannie's half-sister, Clare, has died in what Jeannie feels are suspicious circumstances. Under the assumed identity of governess to Clare's young daughter, Varda, she has come to the island of Langdon's Purlieu to investigate for herself. Once in the house, she cannot understand why the servants seem perpetually frightened. 'Please, miss!' the maid begs her. 'Leave this place! Leave before the blood moon rises over the sea!' Can Jeannie unravel the secrets of the old house, or will she die in the attempt?

V. J. BANIS

BLOOD MOON

Complete and Unabridged

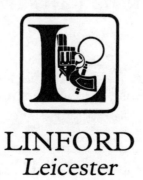

LINFORD
Leicester

First published in Great Britain

First Linford Edition
published 2015

A catalogue record for this book is available
from the British Library.

ISBN 978–1–4448–2590–9

Published by
F. A. Thorpe (Publishing)
Anstey, Leicestershire

Set by Words & Graphics Ltd.
Anstey, Leicestershire
Printed and bound in Great Britain by
T. J. International Ltd., Padstow, Cornwall

This book is printed on acid-free paper

1

'Blood.'

He lifted his fingers closer to the flickering lights, but there was no mistaking the red stains, thick and nearly dry. A wave of revulsion went through him but he thrust it fiercely aside. He had no time now for common shock and horror, not with what must be done.

He raised the lamp again so that its soft light fell upon the child's face. What a paradox it was! Her delicate features were blissfully at ease, softened by the innocent sleep of childhood. She might have been a resting cherub, but for the horror of those red stains.

He turned to the servant beside him. 'Her mother?' he asked.

She did not reply. Only, her eyes grew wider and sadder still.

He handed the old woman the lamp. 'You'll have to wash all that off,' he said in a firm, calm voice. 'Try to do it without waking her. And say nothing about this to anyone, not even that I have been here.'

He hurried away, out of the room. The house was dark but he needed no light to move confidently through its familiar halls, even nearly running as he was. But it was horror and not necessity that made him hurry so. He was too late. The blood had told him that. He knew too where it had come from.

Outside, the blood moon glowed pale in the sky.

* * *

Jeannie Dalton made still another attempt to read the *New Yorker* magazine in her hands. As before, her attention refused to be directed from its own erratic path. She sighed and closed the magazine for what she vowed was the last time, putting it neatly atop the stack on the small table beside her.

Across the reception room, Lou Benner's secretary glanced up from the papers she was thumbing through. Her expression made clear what she thought of people who were too impatient to wait graciously, particularly when they came into a busy attorney's office without an appointment.

Jeannie smiled at her without surrendering any of her obvious impatience. 'Are you sure Mr. Benner knows I'm waiting?' she asked with rigid politeness. The annoyed expression of the woman at the desk had little effect on her. For two of the past three years she had been a secretary herself, not because she needed to work — she didn't — but because she liked it. She knew only too well all of the tricks for discouraging those who tried to intrude upon The Schedule. She had used them all herself, many times.

'I told him you were here,' the woman informed her with some indignation. 'I'm afraid Mr. Benner is terribly busy today. Perhaps if I made an appointment for you . . . ' She had already reached for the appointment book, carefully giving Jeannie no opportunity to object, when the intercom beside her buzzed. She listened for a few seconds and then mumbled, 'Yes, sir,' in its direction.

'Mr. Benner will see you now,' she said

to Jeannie, obviously disappointed to have to make the announcement.

Jeannie suppressed an urge to smile as she stood. On her feet, she looked less childlike than when she was seated. She was small, to be sure, a scant five foot two inches of slender, small-boned woman.

Standing, however, she gave an impression of strength and determination, her shoulders pulled sharply back, her chin held high. Even her walk, as she started without direction toward the door she knew to be Lou Benner's, was the walk of a person who had someplace to go and was quite certain she would get there.

She dismissed the secretary's quick movement to show her the way with a shake of her head. 'I know the way,' she said and, without pausing, pushed open the door that led into Lou's office.

She caught him off guard, an old trick she had enjoyed playing on him in the past and which, even seven years later, made her smile. Half in, half out of his chair, Lou gave her a ferocious glance which became, with alarming rapidity, an expression of shock and finally a wide, toothy grin.

'Jeannie Denver,' he said, all but vaulting the desk in his eagerness to get to her. In the way that he had, though, he paused on the verge of embracing her and instead clasped both her hands roughly in his.

'It's Jeannie Dalton, Lou,' she said, returning his smile. How glad she was to see him.

'So that's it,' he said. He released her hand and took her arm instead, to pilot her toward the leather chair facing his old desk. 'Of course, if I'd known who you were . . . if I had thought for a minute when my girl said the name, you wouldn't have had to wait out there like some blasted saleswoman. That's what I thought you were, you know.'

'It's good to see you, Lou,' she said, seating herself and continuing to smile at him. She had cut herself off not only from her past, but from all feeling too. She had tried to live without caring, or knowing care. But it truly was good to see Lou, good to feel that tremor, like a slow awakening of feeling, within her.

Lou went around his desk and sat down. He gave her a quick but thorough scrutiny, all the while rubbing his hands together as though they were cold. She thought of all those times he had looked her over when she was going someplace or coming home from someplace — boarding school, summer camp, finishing school, rigidly chaperoned tours. Lou was always there to see her off or welcome her home. It had never been Max. Always Lou.

'Dalton,' he said. 'Of course, that's why we couldn't find you. I looked, you know, and before that Susan . . . '

'I know,' she interrupted him deliberately. She did know he had looked for her, and Susan had also, but she did not want to tell him that she had ignored those efforts; had even fled from them. 'Dalton is my real name, actually. You know that, surely. Max never did go through with the adoption, even though I thought for years that he had. So when I left, of course I switched to Dalton.'

'So we couldn't find you.'

'And because I didn't want to have

6

Max's name. I was never really a Denver. It's too bad I never knew my real father. I might have liked him better.'

'You're still bitter.' It was not a question. Lou had grown sober as he studied her.

She avoided his eyes for a moment, uncomfortably facing up to her own guilt. But then she forced herself to meet them. 'Yes, I suppose I am,' she said. 'Max wasn't a very nice man, you know, not even making allowances for nasty step-fathers. I don't remember too much about my mother, of course. I was six, wasn't I, when she died?'

Despite the passage of time, she still faltered on the last word. She smiled bitterly. It was not a word she liked but she had been carefully trained to use it. It had been twenty years and still she could hear Max bellowing at her, *Damn it, she didn't leave. Your mother is dead. Say it. Say, 'My mother is dead.'*

She had learned finally to say it without crying, scarcely flinching. She had to before he would allow her to leave her room. Whatever else, Max had been a realist.

'A lot has happened since then.'

She nodded and said, 'Yes, I know. Quite a lot. Max broke everyone, didn't he? Just as he must have broken my mother. Who was that young woman Allen wanted to marry? What was her name? Elaine, that was it. She might have been a nice person, Lou, despite all the filth he dug up about her family. He drove her to kill herself; shamed her into it. And poor Allen, my own poor brother. God, how Allen hated him for that. I've never quite been convinced that Allen's crash was really an accident. I think Allen might have intended . . . '

She shook her head, attempting to derail herself from this train of thought. She had been over all of it so many times. She knew it led nowhere but to renewed grief. The past could not be rewritten. 'I made up my mind then to leave. The very day Allen died. I had to, Lou, before he broke me the way he'd broken the others.'

'But you liked Susan? She was always genuinely fond of you, you know. She cried when I couldn't find you for her and bring you back.'

8

'Yes.' She let herself see Susan's face for a fleeting moment. Tears came so naturally to Susan, whereas she herself never cried. Not since Max. 'Sometimes we were close enough to be real sisters. I still call her Sis, when I think of her. But she was her father's daughter, Lou. She never could see any of his faults. To her he was still clad in shining armor. If I missed anyone — anyone besides you, I mean — it was Susan. But not enough to come back and endure Max again. I didn't know that she . . . Your letter only reached me last week. I'm sorry I wasn't here . . . '

She paused, not wanting to speak of that and knowing she would have to soon enough.

'Max is dead too,' he said. 'Or did you know?'

'I knew. Some of Susan's letters got through to me, mostly through friends who knew where I was even if they wouldn't admit it to anyone.'

'Just as a matter of curiosity, where were you? Or, you don't have to tell me if you'd rather not.'

She shrugged. 'It can't matter now. I

9

went back to England. That's where I came from, you know, before . . . before my mother met Max.'

'But no accent.'

'That was Max, too. He didn't want me to sound like anything different from him. I had to learn to speak with an American accent. Now . . . ' She shrugged again. 'As for Susan, I knew she married; I got her letter about that, and the one from you when she . . . when she died.' She paused before she said, 'There was another letter, too. I want you to read it, Lou.' She opened her purse and removed the letters, pausing to look at them sadly before she handed them across the desk to him. These were all she had left of Susan . . . Susan, so young and lovely, and so foolish.

Lou read them in chronological order. Jeannie knew them by heart. In the past few days she had read them over and over until she could nearly quote them verbatim. The first letter always gave her a pang with its plea for a reunion.

Susan had been happy when she wrote that letter and it was full, too, of tales about the man she had met and was going to marry — handsome, mysterious and aristocratic Paul Langdon, whose family lived in their own castle on their own island off the New England coast, like medieval royalty. 'You'll love him, Jeannie, I know you will. And think of it, I'll live like a queen. Only, you were always so much more regal than I. Oh, please come home. The doctors say Max will never recover from the stroke . . . '

She hadn't come home, because she had never quite believed that Max would succumb like an ordinary mortal. She had heard, eventually, that Max had died, but by then she had a life of her own and all of that other business was in the past, the past that could not be rewritten. She had been content to let it lie.

Also, although she had never really put it into concrete thought, she had a vague idea that Max would still be there to haunt her, that somehow he had left an impression upon the very air. He surely would not just vanish, like other mortals.

Then, only five months ago, came the second letter from Susan. Nearly six years had passed since the first one. And this one was so very different from the other.

'I was insane to think he loved me. He never did,' Susan wrote. 'It was only the money he wanted. But I've told him I'll give them no more; they won't have another cent. Only, if anything should happen to me, he'd have it then, of course. And he knows that too. Oh, Jeannie, I'm so frightened! How I wish I knew where you are . . . '

Jeannie winced as she remembered. She had not taken it seriously. Susan had always had a tendency to dramatize things, so she had dismissed this as only a fantasy. Five months later, Susan was dead.

Lou finished reading. He returned the letters to their envelopes and handed them back across the desk. 'It was an accident,' he said, meeting her frank gaze. 'The island is a wild place, half boulders and cliffs. Her bedroom opened onto a small balcony that literally hung suspended over the rocks and the ocean. Susan was apparently addicted to powerful sleeping pills. She must have been awake but under the influence of the drugs.

Apparently she went out onto the balcony, notwithstanding that she knew it was unsafe. She lost her balance; perhaps she fainted. She fell against a rotten railing, it broke, and she fell the equivalent of a dozen stories onto the rocks.'

'Are you convinced that's what happened?' Jeannie asked bluntly.

Lou sighed. 'I haven't a shred of evidence to the contrary. Susan had written often of the condition of the house. It was falling apart, even she said so. That's why they wanted her money.'

'Then he did marry her for her money?'

'Presumably so.' He paused for a moment before he went on. 'I went to Langdon's Purlieu myself, after her death. I saw the balcony. The wood was indeed rotten. It would have taken only the slightest pressure to make it break away. I talked to the doctor from the mainland as well. He confirmed that Susan had been heavily addicted to sleeping drugs. He himself had written the prescriptions. And it was he who examined the body after the accident. There was nothing particularly odd

— a wound at her throat that the family never got around to explaining . . . ' He held up a hand to ward off her interruption. 'No, I asked about that too. It looked like a bite mark, but he assured me it was not the sort of wound that could be fatal. Very simply, in his opinion, she died from her fall.'

'What did the authorities say?'

He took a long time to answer. 'The Langdons are the authorities on the island. It's quite outside the territorial limits.'

'I see.' But she did not see.

'There was a daughter, you know.'

Jeannie was surprised. 'Susan had a daughter? No, I didn't know that. Her letter didn't mention it.'

'Yes. She'd be about six now. I didn't see her when I was there. It seems she wasn't well. Probably shock, I suppose, from losing her mother.'

Jeannie thought for a moment. 'That may have been why Susan didn't leave,' she said finally. 'You see, I've tried to think why, if she was so frightened, if there really was any danger, she just didn't go away. I wondered if she *could* go away, even. It is an island, isn't it?'

Lou nodded. 'Yes, I thought of those things too. The family keeps boats, of course. There isn't any regular service. It's off Maine. There's a little town there, Grandy's Landing, but of course no commercial lines serve the island.'

'So she would have been dependent upon the family boats if she wanted to leave.'

Lou shrugged and said nothing, but the answer was apparent. 'Did she leave, ever? Did she go into the town?'

'Most of the family's affairs in town were conducted by the servants or by Susan's husband, Paul, but about once a month she came in with him. She saw the doctor — she'd been awfully rundown, it seems. And she did some shopping. Except the last couple of months before her accident, she didn't come in then.'

'What about mail service? And telephones? Did they have telephones there?'

'Yes, and no. The man who built the place — that would be Paul Langdon's grandfather — spent a fortune to have phones put in. He contracted with the utility people to lay cables to the island, but the service was poor at best. Mostly they depended upon the mail that came and went once a week with the servants.'

Jeannie let her mind digest what she had been told. Could Susan have been prevented from leaving, if she were really frightened? Perhaps, but perhaps not. Surely she could have managed to use the phone during one of its operative periods, or sent a letter more specific than the one she had sent.

It did look as though Susan had only exaggerated the position she was in. Paul Langdon might have married her for her money but Heaven knew there was no crime in that, and it wasn't even particularly unusual. It was a fact of life every woman with a little money faced. And if Susan, vain as she was, realized that fact, or if they quarrelled, she would be likely to imagine all sorts of dire things.

Still, Jeannie could not rid herself of a certain uneasiness.

'What about the money?' she asked aloud. 'If Susan was afraid they might . . . might

16

do something to her to get the money, she had only to change her will, didn't she?'

Lou frowned and folded his hands together upon the surface of his desk. 'Well, now,' he said, 'she did think of that. I got a letter from her some months back. She said she wanted to come talk to me about her will. But that was all she said, no specifics. And of course she never came.'

'What were the terms of her old will?'

'Max's money went to Susan, of course, when he died. I suppose you realize he had disinherited you. Susan's will, the one she made a year or so after her marriage, was quite simple, really. She left a third to her husband, a third in trust for her daughter, and a third to you.'

'How much is involved, all told?' She really had no idea what sort of money Max had possessed, although certainly she knew he had been wealthy. He had never let anyone forget that fact.

'In the roughest terms, about six million each. Some of it's frozen, of course, and it will take several years to get it all converted.'

Twelve million the Langdons got, then,

with the money to her husband and to her daughter. The Langdon family had certainly profited from Susan's accident.

'I don't need or want my share,' she said. 'There's still the trust from my mother. It's nowhere near that kind of fortune, but I'm not poverty-stricken. And I've worked all along, of course. I saw what it's like living with a lot of money. Max's money, anyway. He didn't come by all of it honestly, either; we both know that.'

Lou ignored the remark about Max's honesty, which was surely not news to him. 'Susan must have suspected you would never be found or that you wouldn't want the money if you were. The will provides that if your portion remains unclaimed for a year it reverts to her husband. And if anything happens to the child, that money reverts to him as well.'

For a husband who had married for money, Jeannie thought, and to whom that money had been denied while Susan was alive — she had said in her letter that she refused to give him any more — it must have been quite a frustration. And a temptation.

'Tell me about them, Lou. Did you know them?'

'Only what I was able to find out before the wedding.'

She knew from his slight blush that Susan had not asked him to check up on the family into which she was marrying. She would have been too innocent and naïve to think of that, but he had done so on his own, out of his personal concern for Susan, and for that Jeannie was grateful.

'I met them twice, at the wedding and at Susan's funeral. There's the mother, sort of the dowager queen, and two sons. Ray is something of a professional charmer, if you know what I mean. I don't think he's ever had a thought in his head more serious than which years were the best for which wines. And of course there's Paul, Susan's husband. He was a nice-looking man. He impressed me as a bit old for Susan, and somehow . . . well, hard. I don't know how to express it any better than that.'

Jeannie nodded without comment. She thought she knew what he meant. Susan would have gone for someone like that, older than herself, and hard as a rock. Like Max, who was no longer around to run her life for her. It would never occur to Susan to run her life for herself.

'The family apparently had a great deal of money at one time, old-country money. They came originally from the Balkans. The house on the island was built by Paul's great-grandfather and somewhat modernized by Paul's grandfather, who died fairly young. His son, Paul's father, was anything but a practical man. He and his brother managed to go through nearly all of the family fortune in no time at all. Some of their properties were gambled away, others were sold to pay off debts.

'By the time Paul came into the estate, it was virtually impoverished. There's Langdon's Purlieu, of course, and one or two other pieces of property, but the truth is they're all mortgaged to the ears. I'd guess it would have taken all of Susan's money and then some just to salvage what's left.'

Lou stopped abruptly as though he had remembered something, or realized he had said more than he intended. He went to where a shiny coffee pot sat strangely out of place amid the somber hues and outdated furnishing, and poured two cups, remembering to add sugar to hers. Jeannie took the cup from him and sipped reflectively.

'Paul inherited his grandfather's love of the island,' Lou went on, 'and a strong family pride. He's worked hard to try to keep the estates together and get them back on their feet.'

Jeannie thought of that hard, determined man, struggling to save his family properties, in desperate need of money — and poor, weak-spined Susan, pretty, reckless and rich. It was an ominous juxtaposition.

'I may as well tell you the rest of it,' Lou said more reluctantly. 'There are some family skeletons, from way back. You understand, my investigations were purely superficial. I hadn't time to do anything more thorough, for one thing, and I didn't want Susan to know I was even making an investigation. But in the old country their name makes people clam up nervously. They're not just disliked. They're feared for some reason.'

'You didn't find out what it was?' she asked. *Or,* she added silently, *you don't want to tell me.*

'I don't know exactly. There was some insanity. One ancestor was off his trolley, plain and simple. And there was a great-great-aunt who was burned at the stake in the Middle Ages.'

Jeannie's eyebrow went up. 'Burned as a witch?'

'Not quite. She was accused of being a vampire.'

'A vampire? You mean those monster-movie things that turn into bats?' She couldn't help sounding a bit flippant. She had no faith in things that went bump in the night.

Lou grinned with her. 'In parts of Eastern Europe vampires played the role that witches played elsewhere. That is, they were often the unfortunate victims of fate. The accused was merely a scapegoat for some ugliness — bad weather, poor crops, an untimely death in the neighbor-hood from some not-then-understood cause. Or he was someone disliked, or with a powerful enemy. Most likely this aunt was merely eccentric. In those days, that automatically made you suspect.' He paused and smiled again. 'Come to think of it, I guess things haven't changed much, have they? Anyway, something untoward happened around the village and she took the blame. But you asked for everything I knew, so . . . ' He lifted his hands palms upward.

Jeannie finished her coffee and stood. Lou rose with her. 'What do you plan to do about the money?' he asked.

'I don't know just yet,' she said frankly.

'The townhouse is yours, by the way. Susan specifically left that to you. It's closed up, but functional, if you want to stay there while you're in the city.'

'I think not. I'll be at the Sherry, if you want to reach me.'

He saw her out. The secretary gave her an icy look but Jeannie failed even to notice it. In the lobby the doorman said, in a voice thick with brogue, 'Ah, you'll be getting wet, miss,' but she only smiled at him and tossed her long blonde hair as she stepped out into the light March rain, no more than a drizzle.

She had walked a block or so along Fifth Avenue when she passed a travel agency, its window gaudy with posters advertising Spain and Greece and Switzerland. She went past and then turned so suddenly she almost collided with a man behind her, to whom she muttered an apology. She went back to the agency. A very young, very slender man greeted her and asked what he could do for her.

'I want to go to Maine,' she told him.

'I see.' His tone of voice indicated that he wondered why anyone would want to go to Maine at this particular time, when there were so many places that were wonderful right now — Spain, for instance, or Greece, or Switzerland. 'Any special place in Maine?'

She had to think for a minute. 'Yes,' she said, 'a town on the coast, called Grandy's Landing.'

2

'Grandy's Landing.' In case there were any doubt for whom the announcement was intended, the bus driver gave Jeannie a quick look over his shoulder.

She stood and stretched to get her bag down from the overhead rack. The driver gave her an impatient glance in his mirror but made no move to help her. She deliberately took her time and made him wait while she put on her coat before stepping out into the rain. He was muttering something under his breath when he closed the door after her.

The bus pulled away with a deep rumble and she was left alone on the wet sidewalk outside a building that seemingly did double duty as bus station and dry-cleaning establishment.

She was on what was apparently the town's main street. Grandy's Landing, from what she had seen of it coming in, consisted of little more than a few houses clustered about a sheltered cove which provided docking for several boats.

Which explained why getting here had been so difficult. She had managed, by air and train, to get to the next, somewhat larger town down the coast, but from there to here, only a few miles really, her only option had been that somewhat battered bus. Hard to imagine a town so difficult to reach in this day and age.

Up till now, getting here had been her single goal. Now that she was here, she did not in fact know what exactly she intended to do.

The first thing, she decided, was to get to Langdon's Purlieu. And since that island sat, naturally enough, in the water, she would presumably have to make the trip by boat. The rain was like tiny cold darts hitting her face as she looked around. The ocean was to her right. She started in that direction. She had only the one modest bag. All of those trips to boarding school, summer camp and finishing school had taught her how to travel light.

In three short blocks she was at the

water's edge, looking over the windswept ocean as though she might see the island in the distance. Of course, she could not. What she saw was the several boats bobbing in the waves, but no one manning them.

She retraced her steps to a coffee shop she had passed. It was brightly lit against the day's gloom and damp. The interior was warm and smelled of fresh bread baking. Interesting character types, fishermen, she thought, occupied several of the tables. Most of them looked up and unashamedly scrutinized her as she came in. Strangers were a matter of some interest here, it seemed.

A low counter with stools and a bakery case, now sparsely furnished with home-made buns and rolls, ran the whole length of one wall. She took a seat at the counter and ordered coffee. When it came, she addressed the plump waitress, although she knew the men at the tables were listening as well.

'I wonder if you could help me. I want to find someone to take me to that island out there.' She nodded her head in the general direction of the ocean.

'What island is that, miss?' The waitress's face had become less welcoming.

'Langdon's Purlieu,' Jeannie said.

The waitress looked beyond her at one of the tables. Jeannie could feel all those eyes on her back but she waited for someone to address her.

'No boats going to Langdon's Purlieu,' a masculine voice said from behind her.

She pivoted slowly on her stool. Three men sat at a table against the far wall. It was impossible to know which of them had spoken. All three watched her steadily with impassive faces.

'Oh, I didn't mean just now,' she said, addressing all three. 'But when the weather clears, if someone — '

The man in the middle shook his head, his red beard wagging. 'Not after the rain, either. We don't go there.'

'But what on earth could you be afraid of?'

The faces remained as set as before. 'What makes you think we're afraid?' Red-beard asked.

'Then, if you're not, surely someone could take me across. It's not as far as all that, is it?'

'The Purlieu is private property. Fact is, it ain't even in the country, being as it's beyond the territorial limits. And such as us ain't welcome there. Are you part of the family?'

The unexpected question caught her off guard. 'No,' she answered simply.

He chuckled and exchanged glances with his companions. 'Most likely you wouldn't be welcome either, then.'

Which she thought was probably an understatement. She really ought to have planned ahead a little better. Susan's sister — or half-sister — wasn't likely to find out any more than Susan's attorney had, and she would probably be even less welcome. No, if she was to find out the truth, it would not be as Jeannie Dalton.

Still, before she could find out anything, she had to find a way to get to the island. She looked around at the other tables but they offered her no encouragement. Someone chuckled faintly. No one met her eyes.

Her face burning, she turned back to the counter and her coffee, drinking it down quickly although it was still hot enough to burn her mouth. She left some change on the counter and, picking up her bag, started for the door.

'If it's really important you get to the Purlieu,' the waitress said after her, 'you might look in up at the Kristal Boarding House. I hear there's a young lady there, a stranger like yourself, who's planning to go across.'

Jeannie looked back at her gratefully. Several of the men were giving the waitress unhappy looks.

'Thank you,' Jeannie said and went out, thinking she had certainly stirred up some strong feelings there. What was it, anyway, that all those men felt about Langdon's Purlieu? Fear? Yes, perhaps, but these weren't snivelling little men; they were husky, straightforward creatures who wouldn't be easily frightened. So then, what? New England aloofness? They weren't welcome there, so they wouldn't go? That was probably closer to the truth.

Finding the woman she wanted at the

boarding house wasn't difficult. She had only to ask for 'the visitor' and was sent straight up to a room on the second floor. Probably, she thought with amusement, they automatically assumed that two strangers ought to be together.

The young woman who answered her knock was about her own age and modestly pretty. Just now she looked more than a little ill-at-ease. She gave Jeannie a curious but not unfriendly look. *They haven't been very hospitable to her either*, Jeannie thought and, seizing the opportunity, flashed her friendliest smile.

'May I come in please? I'd like to talk to you for a moment,' she said, and when the woman hesitated, she added quickly, 'It's very important.'

'Yes, all right.' She stepped aside. Notwithstanding her hesitancy, she looked glad to have someone to talk to.

'I've been told you're going across to Langdon's Purlieu,' Jeannie said as soon as the door was closed.

'Yes,' she said cautiously.

'Are you very well acquainted with the family?'

'No, I've never met them, in fact.' The young woman's lonely desire to talk to someone overcame her reserve and she said, 'I've been hired to tutor a child. I'm sort of a governess, that is. It sounds right out of Jane Eyre, doesn't it — off to the lonely castle? I suppose it's appropriately spooky, too.'

'I can't help wondering why a young pretty girl like you would want to take herself off to a place as lonely as this one is reputed to be.'

'Frankly, for money. They're paying me handsomely and I'm in bad need of some money. But you haven't told me yet what your interest is.'

'I want to get to the island, on a personal matter. And it seems it's a little difficult to arrange.'

'Why, nothing could be easier. You could just come over with me. To tell you the truth, I'd be glad to have somebody along, at least for that first landing.'

'Yes, I had thought to suggest that originally.' Jeannie was silent for a moment, thinking. 'How much money do you need?' she asked abruptly.

The young woman blinked. 'Why . . . my mother needs rather a serious operation, you see. Quite an expensive one, I'm afraid. It will take everything we have in the bank, both of us; our savings and everything, and — '

'How expensive?'

'About forty thousand dollars. We've got that, if we pitch everything in, but it will leave us flat broke. So I need the job, and as I say, the Langdons are offering me generous pay.'

'This operation,' Jeannie said, rummaging in her purse for her checkbook. 'Suppose you had the money to cover it, without dipping into your assets? You wouldn't need the job at Langdon's Purlieu then, would you?'

'Why, no, but — '

Jeannie found her checkbook, opened it, and hastily wrote a check for forty-five thousand. 'To cover incidentals,' she said, handing the check over.

'But . . . you must be joking.'

'I assure you, I'm not. Not in the least. Oh, the check is good. If you go to my attorney there, Louis Benner — here's his card — he'll see that there's no trouble in cashing it. And here is five hundred in cash. That will get you back to New York City, and should convince you of my sincerity.'

The young woman sat down on the neatly made bed. 'If what?' she asked. 'What are you expecting in return for all this money?' The young woman gave her a suspicious look.

'Oh. It's simple. I want to take your place on the island.'

'But I couldn't do that.'

'Why not?' Jeannie finished counting out the cash and handed that to her as well. 'You're only here because you need money. You don't know these people so you can't care much about them. Your mother can have her operation and you don't have to spend the summer holed up on a dismal island in the ocean.'

'But it is dishonest.' The young woman had taken the money, but she looked at it indecisively. 'Won't you tell me why this is so important to you?'

Jeannie had seen the temptation in the eyes regarding the money, but this young lady was not to be bought off quite so easily. Jeannie would have to satisfy her sense of honor. She would have to tell at least a part of the truth.

'I can't explain it all,' she said, 'but I can tell you my sister lived on that island, and something happened to her, and I am not convinced that the truth was told about it.'

'Then shouldn't you go to the police?'

'There are no police there, don't you see? This is why I want to get to the island, and why it's best if I go as you rather than myself.'

'But, that sounds as if it will be dangerous. Aren't you afraid?'

Jeannie considered that for a moment before she said, 'I haven't let myself think of that.'

The young woman picked up the check lying on the table next to the bed. 'All right, I believe you,' she said, glancing at the signature, 'Miss Dalton.'

Jeannie laughed. 'How silly. Here I am taking your place as governess, and I don't even know what name I'm to answer to.'

'I'm Cynthia Burke.'

'And I'm Jeannie Dalton. Have they seen a picture of you, by the way; anything like that?'

Cynthia shook her head. 'No. They have my general description, from my letter.'

Jeannie looked at her critically. 'Well, we are about the same height and weight, and even coloration. I don't think they'll suspect anything. They have no reason to suspect a switch of identities.'

'Well . . . ' Cynthia smiled a bit nervously. 'Good luck, then . . . Cynthia.'

Cynthia. *Yes, Jeannie thought, I must remember that. From now on, I am Cynthia Burke.*

★   ★   ★

'Cynthia Burke?' The man's voice was as dark and rough as his appearance.

The real Cynthia was on her way to New York by this time. The rain had stopped. Knowing that someone was coming from the Purlieu to fetch her, Jeannie had brought her things down to the lobby. She was afraid that if they

36

made enquiries at the desk, they might be told a puzzling story about a young woman who came and then left, replaced by another. But, she reasoned, if they saw her waiting in the lobby, a stranger, they would assume she was Cynthia Burke.

Which was exactly what happened. She had been waiting for less than an hour when the tall, gaunt man came in from outside. He wore a slicker and boots, both wet and gleaming. His dark eyes swept the room and settled at once on her, and he came thudding straight across to where she sat.

'Cynthia Burke?'

A moment of panic assailed her. Suppose the manageress heard and contradicted her? She nodded without speaking, afraid to look around to see if she was still alone.

'I've come to fetch you to the Purlieu,' he said. 'These your things?'

'Yes.'

He picked up the case lightly and turned toward the door. For a moment she only stared after him, but when he reached the door she collected her wits and jumped up from the chair, hurrying after him. The manageress appeared at her little cubbyhole as Jeannie hurried by, giving Jeannie a curious look, but Jeannie pretended not to see her.

People on the street watched them pass. She knew they were objects of attention as she practically ran after the tall man. She supposed it was in part because she was a stranger, but no doubt, too, the island and its inhabitants were curiosities to the townspeople, who seemed to be staring at him as much as her.

He looked at no one in return, never turning his head in either direction. People they passed moved aside, casting furtive glances, and she saw more than one window curtain drawn aside.

A large motor launch waited at the landing, dwarfing the little fishing boats. He put Jeannie's case up front. It was an open boat, so that when they started the spray lashed her face and she was grateful for her raincoat.

He had said nothing since those first remarks at the boarding house, and now he concentrated entirely on piloting the boat. She huddled into a corner, trying to shrink away from the cold, wet air.

As they pulled out of the cove, she turned and stared back at the town. Grandy's Landing had none of that quaint charm one associated with New England villages. Still, there was something sad about watching it disappear behind her, seeming to fade into the fog. She had an eerie feeling that she might not see it again. For a brief moment she envied the real Cynthia Burke, by this time safely on her way to New York.

She looked at the back of the man piloting the boat, and wondered what he might do if she told him she had lied to him; that she was not who he had come for.

Probably, she told herself with a grim smile, *he would toss me overboard*. As if in warning, a wave lashed high and spilled over the side into the boat. She pulled her coat closer and looked ahead, in the direction of that mysterious island.

Langdon's Purlieu. What would she find there?

3

Her initial impression was that Langdon's Purlieu was an aggressively bleak place. The first thing she saw as they approached — in fact, nearly all she saw — was rock. Rock, in such profusion that it seemed, even for nature, vulgar. It gleamed eerily in the strange, fog-diffused sunlight like a dark gem set out to crown the ocean's rolling plain.

They came in by a landing carved right out of the rock, massive stone steps rising out of the water and leading steeply upward. The silent man busied himself with guiding the craft to its appropriate spot. Theirs was not the only boat moored there. There were several, ranging from a dinghy to a large yacht that made a dark shadow against the gray sky some distance out from the island.

She remembered that these boats were their chief link with the world. They would be her link with the world too. She found herself pondering an odd question — if she had to leave, what boat would she take, and could she manage it? Not the yacht, certainly, and the dinghy would be too small for the ocean crossing. There was another, smaller launch, and she thought perhaps she could manage that in a pinch.

The boat glided to the dock and bumped gently against rock. The motor sputtered and went silent. They had arrived.

To her surprise, since he had ignored her on the crossing, he gave her a hand and helped her out onto the wet, slick rock. She moved warily away from the water, conscious that in her heels it would be easy to lose her balance.

Something moved above her on the wide steps — a shadow emerging from the others, coming downward. 'Franz, is that you?' a man's voice called.

'*Ja*,' the pilot called back, busy unloading stores from the launch.

'What on earth did you go in for today? I thought . . . ' He came down the steps, almost to where Jeannie stood, before he saw her. When he did, he stopped in his tracks, staring at her in surprise.

This, she knew, had to be Paul Langdon. He was shorter than she had expected, less than six foot by an inch or so. She had anticipated someone tall and slim and elegant. He was thick-bodied and too ruggedly manly to be described as elegant. He was handsome, as Susan had said, but not in a polished way. His face, rather rough-sculptured, seemed to echo the craggy landscape of the island, his features as harsh and arresting as the cliffs towering over them. He did not look like the lord of an aristocratic manor.

His eyes, a unique silver color she had never seen before, fastened on her. They were cold and they inspired fear, but too they made one want instinctively to warm them. 'Why have you come here?' he demanded curtly, those metallic eyes seeming to look right through her. 'This is private property. Visitors are not welcome.'

Her heart jumped. A dozen thoughts flitted through her mind. Did he know she was not Cynthia Burke? Had Cynthia forgotten some snapshot she had sent ahead? Or had he — and this thought had never entered her mind before — had he at some time seen a picture of Susan's sister?

He was standing far enough above her that she had to lean her head well back to meet his gaze. It suddenly occurred to her that this was deliberate on his part. She was being stage-managed. He meant to intimidate her. She gave her damp hair a toss and came boldly up the steps. It surprised him — for a second she saw a glint of something else in his eyes, and it gave her a minute to collect her wits.

When she was on the step with him, and feeling more his match, she said, 'I'm Cynthia Burke, the new governess.'

'New governess? For whom?' He looked genuinely surprised to hear of it.

'I thought for a little girl, although if anyone else feels the need for lessons, perhaps in manners, I'll be happy to extend my services.'

He ignored that sally and turned rudely from her. 'Franz, what do you know of this?' he demanded.

Franz had stopped unloading and stood, head down. Without looking up, he said gruffly, 'The mistress sent me to fetch her from the town.'

Running steps could suddenly be heard above them. Paul Langdon and Jeannie turned together, to see a man and a woman hurrying down toward them.

Here was the aristocracy she had expected. The woman was first down the steps. She was tall and thin and handsome, although well on in years. Despite the fact that she was running, clutching an afghan about her shoulders, a wisp of hair tugged loose by wind and rain, she managed nonetheless to look entirely regal.

The man behind her was younger than Paul Langdon, and Jeannie guessed him to be the brother, Ray. He was the elegant one, and slim; too pretty to be described as handsome, but attractive certainly — the sort of man a woman might want to mother, but not just that alone.

The woman, whom Jeannie took to be their mother, had a look of consternation on her face, but Ray had a twinkle of amusement in his eyes. They brightened still more when he got close enough for a good look at Jeannie. She couldn't help being pleased despite the awkward circumstances.

'You must be Miss Burke,' Mrs. Langdon greeted her, reaching out to clasp her hand. 'I'm Beatrice Langdon and these are my sons — Ray, and Paul, here, I suppose you've already met.'

'Not exactly,' Jeannie said, and to both the men, 'How do you do?' Ray smiled brightly and nodded. Paul ignored the greeting.

'What is the meaning of this?' he asked his mother. He was no more pleasant toward her than he had been toward Jeannie.

'Miss Burke is the new governess,' Beatrice Langdon said in a calm voice, her expression unconcerned — but a tense flexing of her fingers revealed her nervousness in the face of her son's displeasure. 'I've hired her to take care of the child.'

'I think Maria can manage quite well, with help from the rest of us.' He turned to the boatman. 'Franz, I'm afraid you'll have to take Miss Burke back to the landing. If you leave right now you'll have no trouble getting back before evening.'

There was not a word for Jeannie. For a moment she stood in stunned silence. Then the rudeness of her dismissal struck her and her temper flared. 'I'll thank you, Mr. Langdon,' she said, her eyes flashing angrily, 'not to treat me as though I were a piece of misplaced baggage. I have come here over a considerable distance, at considerable expense and inconvenience, and at the request of a Mrs. Beatrice Langdon, with whom I corresponded and who hired me to work here as a governess to her grandchild. I have had to wait for several hours for a storm to end and I have had a long, cold, and wet boat trip over here from the mainland. And now I have been rudely insulted.'

If he were surprised or moved by her outburst he did not show it in his expression, which remained as hard and angry as before, but his eyes changed slightly. They looked at her for a long moment in an inquisitive manner, giving her the impression he did not quite understand her. She could almost have sworn he did not know how she had been insulted. She would not have been surprised had he thrown her off his island, into the darkening water. Probably, in his book, that would be an insult.

He stared for such a long time that her anger burned itself nearly out and was replaced by embarrassment. If she had intended to get on the good side of this man, she was certainly off to a bad start.

He came to a sudden and surprising decision, and made a gallant gesture with his hand toward the steps leading up. 'Forgive me. Of course, you are right,' he said. 'You are entitled at least to something warm and a few minutes of rest. If you'll permit my brother to escort you up to the house, I shall join you there shortly.' A faint smile played with the corners of his mouth but got no further.

'Thank you,' she said.

Ray Langdon, making no attempt to conceal his amusement, took her arm. 'Mother,' he said, gesturing for the older woman to lead the way. She swept by and ascended the stairs before them, back straight, head high.

'Oh.' Jeannie started to follow, and paused. 'My bag.' She thought suddenly that if she carried it up, it would reinforce her intention of staying.

Paul Langdon gave her a look that might have read her thought. 'Franz will see to it,' he said.

There was nothing for her to do but nod and accept Ray's hand again. As they started up, she with reddened face, Paul said after her, 'Be careful of the steps, Miss Burke. They're wet and can be dangerous if you are not familiar with them.'

And, she added silently, *he means I'm wearing silly shoes for an island visit.*

She marched angrily upward, thinking that Paul Langdon was the most incredibly rude individual she had ever met — not to mention one of the most attractive.

At first sight the house looming before them seemed to be nothing more than an extension of the rock of which the island was composed. The steps led to an opening cut in a high wall of stone. Heavy gates stood open and she reflected as she passed through that Langdon's Purlieu had been built as if it were meant to defend itself against attack. And perhaps it had.

They came into a courtyard. In its center three marble naiads laughed and splashed water, while from the fountain's center King Neptune's grim visage reminded her that she might not be altogether welcome here.

'Take Miss Burke into the parlor,' Mrs. Langdon directed over her shoulder. She herself went straight across the courtyard to enter by what was apparently the main entrance, while Ray steered Jeannie through a door to their left.

Although it was only afternoon, it was evening inside the house. The light seemed to shrink from the gray walls and although there were oil lamps flickering along the hallway, they were powerless to dispel the shadows that hung thickly.

He brought her into a small room, busily furnished. A fire burned brightly, adding some warmth and cheer, and old tapestries softened the harshness of the stone walls. It was an odd house, but effort had been made to make it comfortable.

'This is the least funereal of the rooms,' Ray said. 'I hope the house hasn't frightened you unduly.'

'I find it very interesting,' she said, moving instinctively toward the fire. She had not exaggerated at the landing; she was indeed cold and wet and tired.

The look he gave her was both amused and intrigued. 'Yes,' he said softly, 'I can see you are not a woman to be frightened easily.' His mocking smile came back. 'If my brother's temper can't frighten you, I don't suppose anything could.'

'I've been exposed to rudeness and old houses before,' she said, not liking his mocking laughter any more than his brother's sharp tongue. 'Will your mother be in to see me? I should like to discuss my job.'

'If you still have it,' he said. 'At the moment I suspect that Mama and Paul are having a full-scale battle. And if you'll excuse me, I find them most entertaining.

I think I shall go see the outcome.'

'Mr. Langdon?' He had gotten to the door but he looked back at her. 'Who do you think will win?' she asked.

'Who would you bet on?'

After a moment, smiling, she said, 'Myself.'

He grinned back at her. 'So would I.'

But she had lied to him in more ways than one. She was frightened here, and she was not accustomed to men like Paul Langdon, or houses like this one. She shrugged off her wet raincoat, draping it across the back of a chair, and went nearer to the fire, rubbing her arms to speed the circulation.

She found it hard to imagine Susan here in this setting, and easy to imagine that in this bizarre dwelling, one's dark fantasies would fester and poison one's judgment. Was that what had happened to Susan?

As for Susan's husband — Paul Langdon was a man to excite the senses, to disturb one's emotions.

A faint sound behind her made her start and turn. A woman had come into the room; a tiny, shrivelled creature whose face seemed to be composed almost entirely of eyes, in the shade of which her miniature nose and mouth had all but disappeared.

'I have brought you some tea,' she said in a voice as tiny as her features. 'Mr. Langdon's orders.' She carried a tray which she set upon a table near the fire. Jeannie could not help but notice that her hands trembled. Age, perhaps?

She wondered which Mr. Langdon had ordered tea for her and was about to ask, but something about the woman's manner stopped her. It was not age that shone in her wide eyes, but fear. As she straightened from pouring the tea, she slid close to Jeannie. In a voice so small it might have been the flames rustling in the fireplace, she said, 'Oh, leave this place, miss. Leave before the blood moon rises over the sea.'

Then she was gone, as lightly as she had come, leaving a bewildered Jeannie to stare in consternation after her.

4

Jeannie poured herself a cup of the tea and sipped it standing directly before the fire, but the chill within her had deepened.

What did it mean, that whispered warning? The fear that had inspired it seemed genuine. She had a terrible urge to seize her coat and flee this room, the dark halls and the courtyard with its laughing naiads (and what did they find so amusing?), to race down those rough-hewn steps to the landing and the launch waiting there. She did want to be gone before the blood moon had risen — though she had no idea what a blood moon even was.

Suddenly she had the unmistakable sensation that she was being watched. It was so specific that she could not chalk it up to uneasiness and the gloom of the house. She did not even need the sound of furtive movement to confirm the fact.

The movement had come from beyond the open door, from the darkness of the hall. She had a glimpse of something pale moving out of the range of the firelight, going swiftly past the doorway. For a moment there was nothing. Then she heard, very faintly, a thin, muffled laughter as if someone laughed into a hand.

Fear became anger. She did not like being spied upon and liked being laughed at even less. She sat her teacup down upon the tray and strode quickly and decisively to the door.

As she stepped into the hall she had a glimpse of something white disappearing through the next door. Jeannie went straight to it. It stood open upon a dark room. She took a pace or two into the darkness and paused, listening.

Something tried to scurry past her, something small and cloaked in white. Without thinking, Jeannie reached out and grabbed a small hand, holding it fast. Their combined momentum brought them back into the hall.

The lamp hissed and flared and

illuminated the upturned face of a frightened child. For a fraction of a second, Jeannie flashed back in time. It was Susan's face, Susan as a little girl. The past was so vivid that her hand shot out to the stone wall, not so much to get her balance as to assure herself of its reality.

It was the eyes that brought her back to the present. Susan's face had Paul Langdon's silvery eyes. Although they were softer and more trusting than his, they were his eyes beyond question.

In the tension of being here, she had all but forgotten the child Lou had mentioned — presumably the one she was here to tutor. She let out her breath and smiled, relaxing her grip on the small hand. The girl pulled loose and stepped back a pace, but she did not run away again.

'Hello,' Jeannie said. 'You're Varda, aren't you? Susan's little girl?'

She realized her mistake at once. 'How did you know that?' Varda asked, surprised out of her fear.

Jeannie had to suppress the urge to tell

her the truth. It went against her grain to practice deception. She was willing to do it with the adults of this family to find out the truth she was after, but to lie to an innocent and trusting child seemed loathsome.

Of course she had no choice unless she wanted to give herself away. 'A friend told me,' she said, and added, 'I'm Cynthia Burke.'

'Are you going to stay with me and be my friend?' The tone of voice suggested that she very much wanted a friend.

Jeannie hesitated. She herself didn't know the answer to that question yet. 'I hope so,' she said. Then, because she saw this answer was disappointing, she smiled brightly and stooped down so that they were on the same level. 'What will we do together if we're friends?' she asked. 'There must be a great deal to do in a place as big and grand as this one. Can we explore the island together? It's a large one, isn't it?'

Varda shook her head gravely. 'We can't go out onto the island.'

'But why on earth not?'

'Because,' Varda said in a lowered voice, her eyes like silver dollars, 'it's very dangerous. There are dark things out there.'

Jeannie was shocked into silence. Even the child was afraid here, but of what? Dark things waiting beyond the stone walls of this house, waiting to . . . ?

Loud footsteps approached down the hall and suddenly Paul Langdon came around a corner holding a lamp aloft, his wet slicker flying behind him. He stopped short when he saw them, his eyebrows shooting upward.

'What on earth . . . ? What are you doing here?' he demanded of the child.

She put her hands to her face. 'I came to see the visitor,' she said timidly.

He went past them into the dark room and yanked violently at a bell cord. Jeannie heard a tinkling nearby and before it had quite finished echoing, the old servant woman came scurrying into the hall. She too looked shocked to see Varda there.

'Is this how you look after her?' he demanded. 'She's here, with this stranger, unprotected.'

'I am sorry, sir,' the woman mumbled.

'I only turned my back for a minute and she slipped away. Come along, you.'

Jeannie made an effort to keep her temper under control. She knew she should not dispute the father in the child's presence but she was very near to forgetting herself.

'Go with Maria,' he told Varda sternly.

Varda went without a word and without even glancing again at Jeannie. When they had disappeared into yet another room, Jeannie turned to him. 'Mr. Langdon,' she began angrily.

'Will you come with me into the parlor?' he asked.

It caught her off balance and after a blank moment she said, 'Yes,' and followed him into the room she had quitted a few minutes before.

He had seemed to have something important to say to her, but when they were in the parlor it was as if he had forgotten it. He looked at the tea things and went to stand at the fireplace, his back to her, gazing into the flames. She waited too, just inside the room, afraid for some reason to come too near.

After a long silence he said, speaking to the burning logs, 'This is not an ordinary home. We are not ordinary people.'

She could think of no answer to that. After a while he turned around, looking as if he were surprised to see her still there. He stared openly. She resisted the impulse to fidget. He made her feel like a naughty schoolgirl.

'You're not easily frightened, are you, Miss Burke?' he said.

'No, I'm not,' she said, surprised by the statement. His brother had made almost the same remark to her a short time before. The truth was, she had no intention of letting either of them know how frightened she was just at the moment.

'My mother feels that the child needs someone to give her lessons,' he said in a different tone of voice altogether, a business-like voice. 'I have agreed to let you stay on here, to see how things work out. I believe salary and other details have already been agreed upon?'

She nodded, realizing that she had neglected to ask Cynthia Burke what sort of salary she had agreed to.

'I have only one thing to add to what you have been or will be told by my mother,' he said, fixing his eyes on her. 'I do not wish you and my daughter to be alone together. Maria is very busy managing the house for us but we shall try to arrange a convenient time of day when she can be with you while the lessons are given.'

She waited in silence, expecting some explanation for that odd arrangement and hoping as well that he might apologize for his previous rudeness. Neither, however, was forthcoming. After a moment he said, 'Maria will show you to your rooms. I hope you found the tea refreshing. I thought it would be welcome after your journey.'

Before she could thank him he was gone, striding swiftly from the room. She stared after him. All these people moving so quickly, as though pursued by the shadows of Langdon's Purlieu. She even found herself moving hurriedly, wanting to flee from place to place, corner to corner, room to room — but the shadows were everywhere.

Maria was back a moment later, without Varda, her eyes downcast. She did not repeat her previous warning, but motioned silently for Jeannie to follow her. Snatching her raincoat from the chair where she'd draped it, Jeannie followed in her wake. The darkness parted before them, cleaved by the lamp Maria held high, and closed in an eddy behind them.

They went not to Jeannie's room, however, but to Mrs. Langdon's, where she sat embroidering before yet another blazing fire. Her son, Ray, stood near her chair, sipping a glass of wine. He smiled brightly at Jeannie and she was glad to return his smile. He was the only one who truly seemed glad to have her here.

Mrs. Langdon smiled too, if a bit less warmly, and laid aside her embroidery. 'Ray will show you to your rooms in a moment, Miss Burke,' she said, dismissing Maria with a nod. 'I wanted only to welcome you to Langdon's Purlieu and to apologize for the scene at the landing. My son, Paul, did not expect you and he tends to be a little explosive at times, but

I think you will find his bark considerably worse than his bite.'

'I generally avoid getting bitten,' Jeannie said, but she smiled again to show she was not alarmed.

'Very wise of you.' Mrs. Langdon took up her embroidery again. 'In the morning we will discuss your duties. For now you no doubt would like to rest and refresh yourself. Dinner is at eight, Miss Burke, and you will eat with the family. Ray, will you be so kind . . . ?' With a nod, she returned her attention to her needlework.

Ray seemed only too happy to be her escort. She could not help thinking what a dreary sort of life this must be for a young man of his obvious high spirits. At least in his presence, however, the gloom seemed a little less pervasive, and she was grateful he was here. She could certainly not think of him as a threat to anyone. That would require more serious thoughts than she imagined him capable of.

'It's lovely,' she said when he had shown her into the room that was to be hers. Her bag had been brought up already.

'You lucked out,' he said, checking the fire and turning up the lamps slightly. 'It was the only one all ready for a visitor. The past mistress of the house used it as her own for a time. She seemed to want to be away to herself.'

Jeannie stiffened and turned her back so he would not see her expression. This was Susan's room? Her eyes went to the windows. Were those the windows from which she had fallen? The curtains were closed, shutting out what little light might have been permitted to enter.

She went to the windows and pulled the curtains aside, to reveal a tiny balcony — or, rather, what had been a balcony. Now there were only a few broken pieces of wood and railing. The rest had toppled into the sea below. From the window it was a sheer fall, more feet than she cared to estimate, to the rocks and waves below.

'My brother's wife fell from that window,' Ray said in a low voice. He had come to stand close behind her. 'Needless to say, you'll not want to venture outside.'

When she said nothing, he added in a kinder voice, 'If it will worry you, I'll see about having another room readied.'

She shook her head and managed to give him a wan smile. 'No, please don't bother. It's a lovely room and the view is breathtaking. I'd like to stay here, if I may.'

He bowed deferentially. '*Mais certainement*,' he said. 'Dinner is at eight, as my mother said. If you wish anything, you have only to pull this cord by the door to summon Maria.'

'There is one thing,' she said quickly. 'I wanted to ask, what is a blood moon, if you know?'

He gave her a quizzical look. 'What makes you ask that?'

'I heard it in the village and it lingered on my mind. It's not important, of course, but you know how annoying that can be.'

'Yes,' he said. 'As a matter of fact, we have one this evening.'

He brought her back to the window and pulled the curtain aside. It was sunset. The sun was a red ball as it touched the rim of the sea, and the rising moon reflected the red. That heavenly orb was transformed so that it did indeed look as if the moon's surface were stained crimson with blood.

'It only happens from time to time, when the sun and moon are just right toward one another and the ocean. In the old world it is considered an evil omen, a warning of impending doom.'

She looked up at him, but if he meant that to be a warning, he did not show it. His smile was as gay and trivial as before. 'See you at dinner,' he said, and left her alone.

She looked out the window again. The sun had set and the blood moon had risen over the sea. Its surface now was silver again — like Paul Langdon's eyes.

5

They ate in a long hall, served at the heavy carved table by the ever-present Maria and a young girl whose job it was to assist her. Ray was charming and witty and treated Jeannie like an honored guest. Mrs. Langdon was pleasant, but her ever-so-slight aloofness served to remind Jeannie that she was a paid employee. As for Paul, he seemed scarcely aware of her presence.

'I think,' Jeannie said when dinner was ending, 'if no one minds, I shall retire early.' She stood before bringing up a subject that had been on her mind. She knew it risked another flare-up of Paul's anger, and for this reason she asked her question directly of him.

'When I talked to your daughter earlier, she suggested that there might be certain dangers here on the island,' she said. 'Dark things, as she expressed it. I don't mean to be rude but I only wonder if there is anything in particular I should know about?'

'If you follow your instructions and stay in the right places, there should be no danger,' he said, staring back at her.

Mrs. Langdon came to her rescue. 'There are dangers on the island, of course,' she said. 'Some things are especially dangerous for a young girl who might go wandering about unless properly warned, and even for someone older, but there is nothing particularly mysterious about them. You must understand, apart from this house, the rest of the island has been left rather in a natural state. There are snakes, and wild boars, which the men sometimes hunt for sport. There are beaches where the tides come in as swiftly and as dangerously as Mont St. Michel. If you're not familiar with that, I mean that someone on the beach and unaware could be caught in them and swept out to sea before reaching safety.

'So, yes, naturally Varda has been cautioned against going out of the house lest she stumble upon these dangers. As for her description of 'dark things,' Maria has had the chief responsibility for the child since her mother left us. Maria is old world. It is their way to enforce rules with tales of bogeymen.'

'You are not afraid of bogeymen, one hopes,' Ray said, grinning.

'No,' Jeannie said, 'but I should have been most unhappy to go for a stroll and find myself set upon by wild boars or dangerous tides. I ought to have been warned without asking, I think, if you'll pardon my saying so.'

'You ought not to contemplate wandering about the island without permission,' Paul said curtly. 'You are here to teach the child in a room set aside for teaching. You have your own room. You will eat here with us, and Maria will show you around the principal rooms of this part of the house. I see no reason for you to extend your strolling beyond these, if you'll pardon my saying so.'

Her face burning, she turned on her heel and left the room. Maria had come earlier to show her the way to the dining room, but she found her way back with no difficulty, despite the long, dark halls with their profusion of doors.

Back in her own room, she seated herself before the low-burning fire and tried to think what she ought to do now that she was here. She would have to get the family to talk of Susan. In that way, she could put together in her mind a picture of the life Susan had led. That ought to tell her how much of Susan's danger had been real and how much imagined. Certainly, she told herself as a log snapped loudly, it would be easy to imagine danger here, and not such as snakes and wild animals, either.

She was not, however, imagining that someone had been through her things. She had unpacked neatly, putting her dresses in the armoire and the rest in the marble-topped dresser against one wall. She had not closed a drawer on the lace of a slip, as it was now. She had come back to the dresser just before leaving her room and would have noticed it then, that fringe of pink lace conspicuous against the dingy whiteness of the dresser.

She stared at the lace for several long

minutes. It could only mean one thing: someone had searched her room while she was out.

She thought back. She had summoned Maria shortly before eight, and Maria had led her to the den where Mrs. Langdon was drinking a glass of sherry. Maria had informed Mrs. Langdon that Paul was in his study and would join them shortly. No explanation had been offered for Ray's whereabouts, and he had come in a few minutes later, followed soon after by Paul, and they had gone into the dining room together.

Either of the Langdon brothers might have been in her room. She shook her head. No, it wasn't that simple. Maria might have come back here. Or it might have been the man from the boat, Franz, who she had learned was Maria's husband. For that matter, Varda might have come in out of nothing more than curiosity. According to what Maria had told Jeannie, Varda ate in her own room, except on special occasions.

Well, Jeannie thought, there was nothing for anyone to find. Still, she opened the drawer and studied its contents. She never wore monogrammed clothing or jewelry, with one exception. She had a locket with her initials on it. Susan had given it to her years before as a birthday gift, and she wore it almost constantly. She had it on now, in fact, but she had remembered the initials earlier at Grandy's Landing and she wore the locket under her dress.

She opened the second drawer and caught her breath sharply as her eyes fell on the letters from Susan. She'd forgotten about them. She carried them to the light, examining them closely, but it was impossible to tell if they'd been read or not.

'Rot,' she said, tossing them into the fireplace. She watched them curl, smoke, and burst into flames. When they were nothing but ashes, she took the poker and stirred them around until there was no evidence that letters had been burned.

There was nothing more she could do about that, but hope that whoever had searched had not found them, or at least had not read them. She went to bed, and quickly fell asleep.

* * *

The sound of someone crying awakened her. She sat up in bed with a start. For a moment she couldn't think where she was.

Memory came back to her finally — she was at Langdon's Purlieu, the house of stone on the stone island. She brushed her hair back from her face.

It came again: a soft, muffled crying. A child's sobs. For a moment, still dazed with sleep, she thought it was Susan crying, as she often had when they were little. From habit, she got up to go to her.

No, Susan was dead; she remembered that now. And this was no ghost. The crying was real.

'Varda,' she said aloud. She opened her door cautiously. The crying was more distinct. It was not especially loud, but the nature of the house caused it to echo along the passages, amplifying the sound. She started in one direction, listened, then went in the other. Yes, it was this way, she was certain.

She rounded a corner. A flight of steps,

narrower than the main stairs, led upward. She had not brought a lamp and did not wish to go back for one. She put her hand out to feel the cold wall. Its chilled solidity oddly reassured her and she went quickly up the stairs.

The crying came from behind the door at the top and it was unquestionably Varda who was crying. Jeannie reached for the knob and turned it, pushing gently against the door. It did not budge. Then she saw the bolt that held it fast.

It took several seconds before the full implication of that hit her. This bolt was on the outside of the door, not inside. Varda was locked in her room. Bewilderment blended with indignation. This was barbaric, no matter what the child had done to earn her father's displeasure. She reached for the bolt, her fingers touching the cold metal.

Fingers of steel closed over her hand. She was yanked about so suddenly and so violently that she fell against the heavy door. Paul Langdon stood there, dressed in an elegant robe of maroon silk that did nothing to soften his appearance. His face was livid with anger.

'What are you doing here?' he demanded.

Frightened though she was by his unexpected appearance, she managed to say evenly, 'I heard Varda crying and I came to comfort her.'

For a moment she almost thought he would strike her. He seemed to be waging a terrific battle to regain control of his emotions.

'Come with me,' he said finally. He turned, giving her arm a jerk, and started off down the stairs, fairly dragging her along so that she had to half-run to keep up with him. At the open door to her room, he shoved her rudely before him.

'Stay in your room at night,' he said sharply. 'Keep your door locked.'

She managed to find her voice at last. 'I won't,' she said, all too aware that she sounded like a stubborn child. It was difficult to maintain her aplomb when she was being treated like a sack of flour.

'You will,' he said. 'That is an order.' Their eyes met angrily.

He won that contest. She was too angry to think of a retort, which only made her angrier still. She stepped back, inside her room, and slammed her door in his face. And for good measure she sent the bolt crashing into place — the bolt that was where it belonged, on the inside of her door, and not, as with Varda's, on the outside. She bruised her knuckle sliding it home, which did nothing to improve her disposition.

Her fire was out. She pummelled the remaining coals with the poker, a succession of horrid thoughts crossing her mind. The flame that sprang up when she tossed on a log reminded her that the eternal powers had prepared a place for people like Paul Langdon.

6

After the gloom of the night, morning broke golden over the ocean. The water was painted with gilt at the crest of every rolling wave. The rocks below and the stone of the old walls sparkled as though set with countless tiny gems, each blinding her with its brilliance.

The fog and rain that had made the place so dreary the day before were gone, so completely that it seemed impossible they could ever return, and even the shadows in her room were soft and without menace. Standing at her window, Jeannie could almost believe her fear had been the result of fatigue and overworked imagination.

But, no, Maria was frightened too, and had warned her to leave. Varda acted frightened, and certainly her crying had been real enough. And even, she realized in a burst of insight, Paul Langdon was frightened. It was not anger alone she saw in his face, in his silver eyes, but fear. So there was something here, some secret dread that haunted the residents on this island and cast dark shadows over their days and nights.

Someone tapped at her door. She donned a robe and opened the door to find Maria with a tray that held coffee and fresh croissants, the yeasty aroma wafting up to remind Jeannie that she was indeed hungry.

'You are to begin the lessons this morning,' Maria said. The morning sunlight seemed to have cheered her too. 'There is a classroom and I expect that is where you will be most times, but it is my morning to bake and I have orders I must be at hand, so you shall have to make do with the kitchen today, so says the master.' She recited all this as though she too had had her lessons for the morning.

'I'll be down in about forty-five minutes,' Jeannie said. 'If that's all right. Can Varda be ready then?'

'She will be there.' As an afterthought, Maria added, 'She has nowhere else to go.'

Jeannie swallowed that gloomy remark with a mouthful of delicious coffee. Poor child, shut up in this big old house, apparently day as well as night. She ought at least be permitted out into the sunlight.

She decided firmly to make that her goal for the day. She had come here with the idea of learning more about Susan's death, but she could see she had another responsibility, to Susan's unhappy child.

By the time she left her room, she felt sure that the others would be downstairs, and her curiosity was gnawing at her. With a quick look around, she hurried up the narrow stairs that led to Varda's room. The bolt was back this morning and the door opened to her touch.

It was the prettiest room she had seen in the house. Susan, or someone, had taken great pains to create a delightful room for a little girl. The gray walls were covered with hangings and prints from Mother Goose, Alice in Wonderland, and other children's classics. The windows on two sides were carefully and securely screened, but an abundance of pink ruffles made the room completely feminine.

The room shared an oddity with Jeannie's, however — a lack of mirrors. She'd had to make do this morning with the mirror from her purse. On reflection, she could not remember seeing any mirrors anywhere in the house.

A sleeping pallet lay near the hearth. She went closer and saw the robe that Paul had worn at their confrontation last night. So he was not such an ogre as he tried to seem. He did indeed try to comfort his daughter, even to sleeping here on the floor of her room when she was disturbed. But then why have her locked in?

She picked up the robe. It smelled faintly of its wearer. She had a sudden, shocking sense of his presence and of his intense magnetism. It was so vivid, she dropped the robe and, frightened by what she had felt, she hurried out of the room and down the stairs.

Varda was waiting for her in the kitchen. This was a big, old room with wooden tables and benches, open hearths and vast ovens. Maria energetically kneaded dough at one of the tables. Varda sat at another, a row of books before her. Her smile when she saw Jeannie was shy but eager.

'In my prayers,' she said after their greetings, 'I prayed you would be allowed to stay, so I would have someone to talk to me.'

'Then you must have been a good girl lately, because your prayers were answered. Have you been a good girl?'

'I guess so.' Varda lowered her eyes. 'Only, sometimes I get frightened.'

Jeannie's heart went out to her. She cast a glance at Maria, who was occupied for the moment. 'There's no need for you to be frightened anymore,' Jeannie said in a lowered voice, 'because I'm here now. That's why I came, so that I can see no harm comes to you. Do you believe that?'

Varda gave her a long, agonizing look, but at last she smiled faintly and nodded.

'Good,' Jeannie said more cheerfully. She did not want to dwell on that morbid subject. She picked up one of the books. 'Can you read this?'

'A little bit.'

'Well, let's see how you do with it, all right?'

They read for nearly an hour. Varda was obviously an intelligent child but she had just as obviously been neglected. She began falteringly but learned the words quickly and had no difficulty retaining them or understanding their meaning when it was explained to her.

They worked next on her alphabet. They had been at this a short time when Varda's father appeared, stopping just inside the door to watch them.

The lessons had been going well and Varda had warmed quickly to Jeannie's genuine interest in her. They had even been laughing when he came in, but as if in silent agreement, they both grew sober in his presence.

'I think,' Jeannie said shortly, 'we shall stop here and ask Maria for some lunch.' Paul turned as if to go out. 'Mr. Langdon?' she said.

'Yes?' He looked less formidable this morning than he had the night before.

'I wanted to ask . . . ' She paused,

81

wondering how to make her request without incurring his wrath again. 'It's such a lovely morning, I was hoping you would let me take Varda for a walk along the beach. I think it would do her good to be out of doors.'

'The beaches can be unsafe for one who is not familiar with them.' There was no sign of anger but there was no warmth either.

'Yes, I remember. I thought perhaps you might be willing to accompany us.'

He looked genuinely surprised. 'I'm afraid I have a great deal of work to do this morning.'

She was not prepared to give up so easily as that. 'A little fresh air and sunshine might do you some good, too, you know.'

He came very close to returning her smile and she almost thought he was going to accept the invitation. But his smile never quite came. 'I'll ask my brother to accompany you,' he said instead. 'He has little enough to occupy him and I think he won't mind.'

She had gotten what she told herself

she wanted, but she couldn't help feeling vaguely disappointed. On his way out of the room, though, he turned back once again to say, 'Perhaps it would be good if you brought some of the sunshine and fresh air back with you.'

'I will if you'll let me,' she said, and was immediately embarrassed by the remark. It could be too easily misinterpreted. He did not reply, however, and went out.

She and Varda lunched in the kitchen — a thick, rich soup that tasted of game, with hot bread that Jeannie did not have to be told was fresh from the oven. Afterward, Maria took Varda off to change and Jeannie went to her own room for her raincoat and a scarf.

Ray was waiting when she returned to the kitchen. He brushed aside her apologies for disturbing him. 'It's no imposition to escort two lovely ladies for a stroll,' he assured her.

They came out into a courtyard and Jeannie made a mental note to find out if this were off-limits. On days when Ray was not free to accompany them, perhaps she and Varda could get some air here.

The sun was pleasant but it was winter still and the sea air was cutting. Varda was so happy to be out of doors that she seemed oblivious to the cold. She ran ahead and repeatedly had to be told to wait for them.

They came out of the courtyard on the opposite side of the house from the landing and for the first time Jeannie saw something of the island. It looked smaller than she had imagined but she had to remind herself that she had nothing by which to measure the distance to the peak which Ray informed her marked the opposite end.

'It's about four miles long,' he answered her question, 'and not quite two across at its widest point.'

The island was slightly crescent-shaped, the two ends higher than the rest. The house was built on the narrow peak at the south end. A narrow spine of land was the only link with what, she realized belatedly, at one time had been another house, its crumbling walls long since collapsed.

'Originally,' Ray explained when she

asked about that, 'it was the servants' quarters — we had more servants then, of course. But over time the land eroded. That house was built on softer rock than where the house proper stands, and about twenty years ago a series of hurricanes finished off the causeway. It would have cost a fortune to connect the two buildings again, so that one was allowed to fall into ruin. We haven't got a fortune, you see.'

'You live well,' Jeannie pointed out.

He led the way down a path, breathtakingly narrow, squirming around the face of a cliff with nothing visible below but water. She could understand why she had been warned of danger for the unknowing, and she kept one hand on Varda, walking between them.

'My brother married some money,' Ray said frankly. 'So we were able to get some of the furniture and boats out of hock. You should have seen us before that.'

Jeannie was glad he was ahead of her just then so he couldn't see her excited expression.

'Strange,' she said to his back, 'I get the

impression he was fond of his wife.'

He shrugged. 'I suppose he was. He probably convinced himself he was in love with her. That would be his style.'

The path widened suddenly and they were upon a narrow strip of beach. He helped them over a rock formation, where another, wider section of beach lay between this wall of rock and the steep bluffs. It was like a sandy basin, cut off from the sea, and seeming lower.

'The tides don't really come in any faster here than elsewhere,' he explained, 'but the rocks there hold the water back until it's nearly full tide. Then it comes rushing over almost at once. If you were caught here then, you'd suddenly find that you were completely cut off. Long before you saw the water spilling over these rocks, the paths out of here would be submerged.'

She shivered slightly and stared at the steep cliffs. There would be no escaping up them, either. Trapped here was trapped forever.

'There's no danger now, though,' he said. 'Not from the tides, at any rate.'

Varda began at once to search for seashells. Ray led Jeannie to a large boulder and gallantly brushed it free of seaweed before she sat down.

'Has Varda's mother been gone long?' she asked as casually as she could.

'A few months.'

'How did she die?'

'I thought I said last evening. She fell from that balcony outside your room.'

'Yes, but . . . if she knew the balcony was unsafe, why did she go out on it?'

'Why did you come here if you knew there was danger?'

Her heart skipped a beat. He was watching her closely.

'Why should I know there was danger here?'

'You spent time in town. You must have asked someone about us, about the island. We don't enjoy a very good reputation there.'

'Oh?' Then, to divert him, she smiled mischievously. 'Perhaps you've given the village maidens some cause for bitterness.'

He grinned. 'Perhaps I've given some

of them cause for joy.'

She laughed and was relieved when he laughed too. Quite unexpectedly he took her in his arms and kissed her full on the lips. She did not resist. In fact, it was rather a pleasant kiss. Those things he had troubled himself to learn, he had learned well.

But there was nothing serious about it, neither in the giving nor the getting. She had an impression it was only a matter of form with him.

'Varda,' she murmured when he was about to kiss her again, and he gave it up without any apparent unhappiness.

'What was the young Mrs. Langdon like?' she asked after a time.

'Pretty. Insipid. Neurotic.'

Jeannie bridled but she had to hide her resentment. 'Wasn't she a good mother?'

'No,' he said frankly.

'Surely you don't mean she was cruel, or anything like that?' If he tried to say Susan had been cruel to her daughter, she would know he was lying.

'As a matter of fact, she was,' but he added quickly, 'not intentionally, of course. I don't mean that. She was just too much of a child herself to make a good mother. She played at being a wife and mother and when things didn't work out as she had fantasized, she refused to accept them. When my brother wouldn't be the fairy prince, she decided he must be the toad.'

Jeannie sat in shocked silence. Her first reaction had been anger, dangerously close to erupting, but almost at once she realized he was telling the truth. It was Susan he was describing, with her fantasies and her childishness and her refusal to accept reality.

'It must have been very difficult for her daughter,' she said aloud. She wanted then to make up for Susan's shortcomings. She looked across the sand to where Varda was silently amusing herself, and decided she wanted to try to be the mother Susan hadn't been.

'I suppose it was,' he said. 'I don't know much about kids. My brother fusses over her plenty, though. Lord knows he doesn't pay that kind of attention to the rest of his family.'

He said something more, something complaining, but she wasn't listening. Another thought had flashed through her mind, illuminating it like a bolt of lightning. She also wanted to be the wife that Susan had not been to Paul Langdon.

7

The shock of her realization left her shaken. Even Ray noticed. 'What's wrong?' he asked.

'Nothing.' She slid off the rock.

'You looked for a moment like you'd seen a ghost.'

'Perhaps I have.' She spoke more sharply than she had intended. She was angry with herself and wanted to take it out on him, but she was immediately ashamed of that impulse too. 'I'm sorry, Ray,' she said. 'I was remembering something about my stepfather.' *And how much your brother is like him*, she added silently. It was true, they were alike. Max had been handsome and mysterious, aloof and ruthless, a hard man — but her mother and Susan had both loved him very much.

She had resented that fact because she had unconsciously realized there was another side to him too, a very small part of himself in which were concentrated all his gentler aspects, all of his love, and in which he was vulnerable. He showed that side only to those of whose love he was the most certain, and she had never belonged to that elite.

Paul Langdon was like that as well, and because she had seen a glimpse of that other side in him, she loved him. It was not a love that needed romanticizing. She needn't imagine him any better than he was. One had to take a man like this for what he was.

If his wife had been murdered . . . She left that thought unfinished.

'I think we had better be starting back,' she said.

Either Ray did not notice her newly subdued manner or tact prevented his mentioning it. On the return walk he chatted about the island. 'Do you ride?' he asked as they climbed the path.

'Yes, why?'

'Since you don't frighten easily, you might enjoy one of the island's more adventurous pastimes.' He gave her a quick smile over his shoulder. 'Have you ever hunted wild boar?'

'No.' After a moment's thought, she laughed and said, 'But I think I'd love it.'

'Then we shall arrange a hunt soon,' he said, pleased with her enthusiasm. 'The Langdons are masters of the sport; you'll see.'

'I'm a Langdon,' Varda said. 'Can I come too?'

Jeannie nearly said no, but Ray answered before she could. 'Of course, little one. It's time you earned your colors.'

'Her father may not approve,' Jeannie said.

'He protects her too much. She'll wind up a helpless ninny instead of a Langdon.'

She started to object — but in a sense he was right. Whatever it was Varda was being protected from, the job was too well done. It was not healthy for a child to be constantly 'guarded', kept indoors, never allowed to take the risks natural to childhood. Childhood wasn't just about skipping rope; it was falls in the dirt and skinned knees as well.

As they neared the house, Varda, no

93

longer confined between them on the narrow path, challenged them both to a race. Ray and Jeannie laughingly ran after her, careful to let her remain ahead.

They ran into the courtyard in a burst of noise, all laughing and shouting at once. Out of breath, Jeannie dropped onto a seat on the rim of the fountain. She threw her head back, tossing her hair out of her eyes, and saw Paul watching them from a window.

She could not tell if he approved or disapproved of their boisterousness, but his sober countenance only increased her amusement. Trying to hide her laughter behind her hands, she ran after Varda into the house.

Paul's only comment came at dinner that evening. 'You're a cheerful sort of person, Miss Burke,' he said.

'Yes, I am.' She waited for him to say more, but he only offered her another glass of wine.

She did not want to tax his generosity, and so she waited a few days before making another request, again at dinner.

'I've been wondering,' she said, 'if

94

Varda and I might not spend part of our days in the courtyard.' She saw a scowl begin on his face and added, 'It's surely quite safe there, and Maria could watch us from the kitchen windows.'

He considered this for so long she felt sure he was going to refuse, but instead he said, 'Very well. But stay in sight of the kitchen.'

'We will,' she promised. She smiled down at her plate, and when she looked up, it was to discover that he was studying her once again. He did this often, as though there were something odd about her that troubled him but that he could not quite make out.

'My daughter is very fond of you,' he said, to her surprise.

'Thank you. I'm fond of her as well. She's a lovely thing, and very bright.'

His face changed. A look of great pain flashed across it and was gone almost at once. He put a hand briefly over his eyes and she could not help thinking he was trying to blot out some phantom vision of his own. In a moment he sighed, removed the hand and returned his attention to his food. After that he was silent and morose for the rest of the meal.

She knew that despite his strange behavior toward her, he was inordinately fond of his daughter. Night after night she heard sounds she had learned to recognize. Maria took Varda to her room each night and bolted her in. And each night, her father stole from his own room, climbed the narrow stairs, and slept on the pallet by his daughter's hearth.

Each night she heard the grating of the key as he locked himself in that room with Varda. It was a mystery. If he was there to protect his daughter, from whom was he trying to protect her? And if that were the explanation, why a bolt on the outside of the door?

★   ★   ★

The very day after the use of the courtyard had been granted them, they sat in the warm sunlight there. Varda had brought her coloring book and crayons.

'Which picture should I color?' she asked, thumbing through the pages.

'Why, any one you like.'

Varda stopped at a page. 'Here's one of a pretty lady.'

Jeannie smiled approvingly. 'She looks like a fairy princess.

'She looks like my mother,' Varda said, studying the picture.

Jeannie caught her breath. Varda had never talked about her mother, and Jeannie was unsure now whether to encourage or discourage it.

'That's nice,' she said. 'Why don't you color that one then?'

She got up and strolled around the courtyard to calm her nerves. From the gate she watched Franz doing something to the motor of the launch. She had learned that Franz and Maria had been with the family since they were very young. They had come here with the Langdons from the old country, where the family had once maintained several houses.

Ray had hinted that Franz had committed some crime which might have sent him to prison, but his punishment had been thwarted when the Langdons brought him here, beyond the reach of that law. It had left him slavishly devoted to the family, especially to Beatrice.

Jeannie wished she could talk to him or his wife about the dark secrets that supposedly haunted the Langdon past. But she rarely saw Franz and when they did meet he offered nothing more than a grunt in answer to her greetings. She had a feeling that he resented her presence here, though she could not think why that should be.

Maria had never repeated her ominous warning and now remained completely reserved toward Jeannie.

There was no one else she could question. There was a girl who came twice a week from the village. She never stayed the night and seemed frightened of her own shadow. Once Jeannie had approached her, thinking to engage her in some conversation, but the girl had literally fled from her.

Maria appeared at the kitchen window and called them for lunch. Jeannie sent Varda ahead to clean up while she collected the books and crayons. When she picked up the coloring book, she stared at it in dismay. Varda had painted the woman in the picture a vivid blood red from head to toe. Jeannie tore the page out and when she went in, she tossed it carefully into the kitchen fire, but the red figure haunted her for days.

One other incident occurred to add to her uneasiness during this otherwise quiet period. Since she'd come here, she'd always worn her locket under her blouse, but somehow taking it off one evening, she managed to break the clasp.

She wrapped it carefully in a handkerchief and put it in the far corner of a drawer. She had made up her mind she would ask permission to go into town in the near future, and she would be able to get the chain fixed then. Meanwhile, it would surely be safe in her drawer, and anyway there was nothing else she could do with it short of tossing it into the ocean.

It was three days later before she discovered that it was missing. She removed everything from the drawer and then emptied the other drawers as well, thinking she might have been mistaken over which drawer she had left it in, but it was truly gone.

She could not ask the Langdons about the locket without calling attention to it if it should be found. Varda might have found it in some way and taken it as a souvenir of their friendship. Or Maria might have come across it while she was cleaning and, seeing the broken clasp, meant only to have it repaired. Surely, though, either of them would have mentioned it.

She spent an uneasy evening. Several times during dinner she nearly mentioned the missing locket, only to check herself each time.

'Aren't you feeling well?' Beatrice asked her. 'You don't seem yourself this evening.'

'It's nothing,' Jeannie assured her. 'I think I read too much this afternoon. I seem to have a slight headache.'

She excused herself after dinner and went to her room. As though expecting some miracle to have occurred, she went straight to the dresser and opened the drawer which had held the locket.

The miracle had happened. The locket

was there, wrapped in the same handkerchief, and tucked back into the same corner. The clasp was still broken.

After a moment she took the locket to the window overlooking the ocean and threw it far out, so it would clear the rocks and land in the water.

Locking the barn after the horse is stolen, she told herself glumly, closing the window. She wondered who had taken the locket — and why they had brought it back.

★　★　★

She had forgotten Ray's suggestion of a hunt. It was Paul who brought it up again. 'My brother tells me you would be interested in a boar hunt?' he said one evening at dinner.

'Yes, I thought it might be exciting.'

'It can be. Have you hunted before?'

'No, but I ride well. Anyway, I plan just to stay out of the way and watch.'

'That might be difficult in a boar hunt,' he told her, with a hint of a smile. 'However, if my mother will go along to keep an eye out for you, I think it might indeed be rather an exciting experience for you. Mother?'

Beatrice showed such enthusiasm at this suggestion that she might have been twenty years younger. 'I should love it,' she said with the fervor of a devotee. She turned to Jeannie with flashing eyes. 'We used to hunt regularly. The boar hunting here on the island is the best hunting outside of the Balkans.'

Jeannie was surprised. It would not have occurred to her that this aloof and regal creature who spent her evenings quietly embroidering would have any interest in what sounded like an adventurous pastime.

'Oh,' she said, suddenly turning her attention back to Paul, 'but aren't you coming too?'

His lips had already formed the negative answer, but he hesitated. Again a faint smile played upon his lips and his eyes turned from silver to mercury.

'Would you like me to accompany you, Miss Burke?'

She had a feeling he was teasing her.

Her cheeks reddened but she met his gaze evenly, refusing to look away.

'Yes,' she said, 'I would like it very much.'

For the first time she heard him laugh, a rich full sound that made her heart beat faster. He tossed down the last of his wine in an enthusiastic gesture. 'Then I shall. We'll ride tomorrow. Ray, see that Franz has the horses ready at dawn.'

'Your daughter wanted to come too,' Ray said.

Paul grew sober again. 'No, that's out of the question.'

The room fell silent, the sense of excitement fading.

'I wish you'd change your mind,' Jeannie said. 'About Varda. She could ride with me and you know I'd protect her with my own life if it were necessary. The poor dear has so little fun.'

'She is right,' Beatrice said.

'Anyway,' Ray chimed in, 'it's criminal to think of a Langdon growing up without hunting. It's against all tradition.'

Paul seemed not to notice their remarks, however. It was Jeannie he continued to watch. 'Very well,' he said directly to her, 'perhaps you are right. But it won't be necessary for her to ride with you. I haven't completely neglected my daughter, Miss Burke. She rides quite competently.'

8

Maria woke her before dawn, and shortly after, Beatrice Langdon came in, before Jeannie had even finished her coffee. Jeannie was embarrassed to be found still in her bedclothes, while the family matriarch was already dressed and obviously waiting to ride. This morning her enthusiasm had cancelled out her aristocratic reserve and she spoke to Jeannie not as an employee but as a fellow rider.

'I've brought you a cape,' she said, handing it over. 'You'll find it infinitely more comfortable for riding than that coat you usually wear.'

It was also infinitely more elegant, a long full cloak of leather, lined with fur. The collar was tall and fastened at the throat with a golden chain so that the garment fell behind, out of the way of action.

It was a hunter's cloak and she felt wild and adventurous in it. She had inclined toward wearing the slacks she had with her but the cloak negated that choice. She realized — fortunately, before joining the others — the Langdon women were not the trouser sort.

When she came down she wore a plain white blouse and a full pleated skirt that was warm and graceful and gave her all the freedom of movement she would need. Ray signalled his approval with a whistle. Paul said nothing but Jeannie thought she detected approval in his eyes too. The men were dressed in riding pants with boots and leather cloaks over white silk shirts.

There was a delay while the family argued about Jeannie's walking shoes, the best her limited wardrobe offered. 'The land is marshy,' Beatrice explained. 'The reeds can be very cutting. Your bare legs would look like ground meat by the time we got back.'

Maria was sent to fetch something better, and when they went out into the cold dawn air Jeannie wore elegant but sturdy leather boots that came nearly to her knees.

It was the first time Jeannie had seen

the horses, all of them magnificent beasts. Ray rode a spirited black stallion and Beatrice a handsome roan. For her there was a chestnut that she suspected had been chosen because of his placid nature, and for Varda a Shetland.

Easily the most magnificent of the lot, however, was Paul's mount, a silver stallion — neither white nor gray, but actually silver in color, so that he seemed to match the gleam of Paul's eyes.

They watched Jeannie carefully as she mounted, but she had ridden since she was younger than Varda and she had full confidence in her ability. Franz joined them outside the courtyard and with Paul in the lead, they set off.

At first Jeannie kept a close eye on Varda, but her concern soon vanished. Paul was right, his daughter was entirely competent. She looked every inch the born rider, and Jeannie felt as much pride as if Varda were her own child and not just her niece.

Paul followed a trail Jeannie could not even distinguish, the land sloping gently downward. The morning sun played tag with the lingering mists of night. Jeannie's cheeks tingled with the cold and her breath made little clouds in front of her. She was grateful for the heavy cloak that fell warmly about her.

They reached the lowland. In summer this would be almost a swamp. Even now the spring grass was high and thick, and their progress was slow. Though this was a relatively small island, she guessed it would take a full day to travel around it.

Beatrice had been riding ahead with her sons, but now she dropped back alongside Jeannie.

'There's a rigid protocol to hunting boar,' she explained. 'It's what makes it the most exciting form of hunting, and also the most dangerous.'

'Are boars all that dangerous? They look fairly harmless in pictures.'

Beatrice hooted. 'Don't think that way today, my girl, or you'll wind up minus a limb. Boars are incredibly fast and, unlike a lot of fast animals, smart and agile. And their tusks are razor-sharp. They actually sharpen them on trees and rocks. I've seen a boar take off a man's leg with a motion that looked like nothing more than a gentle nuzzle. They'd go through those boots you're wearing like paper.'

Jeannie looked around the group. 'But no one's carrying a gun,' she said. All three of the men carried long lances and she had seen that Paul wore a hunting knife at his belt, but she had supposed 'hunting' meant guns.

'No guns. That's the way it's done, the same as in the Middle Ages. When a hunter goes after a boar — and only one man can take on the beast — he gets one thrust with a lance. It's almost impossible to kill the animal that way, though. Unless you're awfully good with the lance, it's hard even to wound him very badly.

'One thrust, and then the man has to dismount and go after the animal on foot, with a knife. And the wound may only have enraged the beast. It tests a man's courage to get down into the grass with an animal like that.'

She took a look at Jeannie's frightened face and gave vent to her amusement with another loud laugh. Then, with a sudden wild yell, she was off at a gallop. They were crossing a flat, relatively clear stretch and she rode wildly for the horizon.

With a yelp of his own, Ray was after her. Jeannie watched mother and son racing fiercely, silhouetted against the morning sky.

Paul, intent upon the trail, did not join them. Varda watched the galloping pair with excited eyes and Jeannie knew she yearned to join them. She caught the child's eyes and gave a firm shake of her head.

They paused at midmorning. Thus far they had seen no pigs, but no one seemed discouraged. Paul took a wineskin and held it high as the Spanish do, squeezing its base, facing the wind, so that the wine poured and splashed into his mouth as though from a fountain.

Ray did the same, but Jeannie followed Beatrice's example and drank from the silver cup Paul offered her. The wine was young and strong, and dispelled the body's chill. When she mounted again, she felt lightheaded.

They spotted a boar at last. It broke from the brush not far ahead. Jeannie reined in her horse, calling Varda's name in a low, tense voice. Paul, still in the lead, signalled with his hand for Ray, and at once Ray had broken, racing toward the beast on his stallion.

The boar, large and black, was more formidable than what Jeannie had imagined from pictures. Its tusks curved wickedly and its eyes gleamed. It did not, as she expected, flee, but instead attacked its attacker, charging defiantly toward man and horse.

Ray reined his mount to the right, hanging far out from the saddle, and stabbed with his lance as the beast rushed by within inches of his arms. The weapon broke, its point buried deep in a shoulder. Beatrice cheered. It was a good strike.

The animal stumbled but was on its feet again. Just as swift, Ray leaped from his horse. He ran to the left, but suddenly he lost his balance, his foot catching on something hidden in the matted grass.

He fell, and the boar charged. Jeannie clamped a hand over her mouth to stop her scream. Paul did nothing to save his brother — but of course, she reminded herself, the rules forbade it.

Ray rolled aside and as he did, the hand with the knife traced a graceful loop in the air — drawing the tusks up, swinging around them, and across the throat. Jeannie saw a splash of red. The beast ran for several yards before he faltered, staggered and fell. He snorted and pawed the ground but it was obvious he was done for. Ray got to his feet and went to where the boar still kicked. Another slash of the knife finished the job.

'Bravo,' Beatrice cried, clapping her hands.

Jeannie's horse shook his head nervously at the scent of blood. Franz came forward to take care of the carcass and Ray mounted again, looking at Jeannie for approval. She laughed with excitement and beamed at him.

'It's thrilling, isn't it?' Varda cried, her face flushed, and Jeannie yelled back, 'Yes.'

Paul's prey, when they spotted him, was further off, across a clearing. Almost at once the boar spotted the rider charging toward him. Paul raised his lance for a strike, expecting the beast to return his charge.

Instead, the boar veered and charged toward the women, heading straight for Varda. Jeannie screamed and the Shetland reared.

There wasn't time for Paul to chase it. He made a desperate throw with the lance. It made a surface cut on the animal's side, scarcely drawing blood, and fell free. It was enough, though, to make the animal change paths again. This time it crashed into the dense undergrowth beside them. In a moment Paul was off his horse, running for the wooded area.

'He can't chase him into that,' Jeannie said, horror-stricken. 'That beast's barely scratched.'

'He's got to,' Beatrice said, her own face pale. 'It's a matter of honor. You stay here with Varda.' She and Ray followed Paul on horseback, crashing through the brush in his wake. In a minute they were out of sight, although Jeannie could hear them yelling to one another.

She decided maybe it was a little too

exciting for her blood. She slid from her saddle, glad to stretch her legs for a minute. Varda brought her pony around.

'Daddy said we weren't to dismount without orders,' she said, eyes wide.

'I suppose you're right.' She had scarcely said the words when Jeannie heard a sound like faint thunder. The grass just off to the side swayed and parted as if cut by a scythe, and she heard a soft grunting that sounded deceptively harmless.

Suddenly there he was, a wild-eyed boar with gleaming tusks, staring at her from not more than twenty feet away. She had let go her reins and now the frightened chestnut neighed and reared, and fled.

In almost the same second, the boar snorted and charged straight at her.

It must have been over in a few seconds, yet it seemed to last an eternity. Everything moved in slow motion, like a trick sequence in a movie.

She was helpless before the charging animal. She had time to realize that, and to realize that she could never outrun him to safety.

She had time, too, to see Paul burst

from the brush after him, his face a mask of horror. She even saw Ray riding hard toward her, and time enough to know that he could not reach her soon enough. And all this while, Varda screamed at the top of her childish lungs.

Jeannie moved at the last possible instant — not through any skill of timing, but only because that was the first she was able to make her body respond. She threw herself sideways in as good an imitation as she could manage of what she had seen Ray do. She heard rather than felt the cutting of leather and of flesh, and realized as she rolled over and over on the ground that he had caught her leg with one of those razor-sharp tusks.

Sky and grass tumbled alternately past her and then she was lying face down, sobbing, knowing that if he came again she wouldn't be able to evade him.

Something grazed her arm, but it was not tusks; it was Ray seizing her, turning her so that he could look into her ashen face. In another moment Beatrice had ridden up, staring down at her with frightened eyes.

'Paul,' Jeannie said faintly, struggling free of Ray's embrace. But Paul was already running toward her. Beyond him she had a glimpse of a black carcass. His arms was bleeding profusely, staining the grass. He must have tackled the beast headlong, risking all in one reckless leap — but when she saw his face, she understood why.

He knelt and took her wordlessly in his one good arm, crushing her to him. She clung to him weakly and let herself cry at last, burying her face in his shoulder. They said nothing. It wasn't necessary.

She remembered, finally, his wounded arm, and where they were, and that the others were watching. She sniffled and rubbed a hand over her eyes and pulled away from him. Not until then did she remember that she was hurt herself. One black boot was stained red, slashed open from ankle to knee.

She gave Ray a wan smile. 'I'm afraid I still need a little practice at that sort of thing,' she said.

He laughed with relief. 'You were magnificent.'

'A born huntress,' Beatrice agreed, real respect in her voice as she eyed the wound.

'I couldn't have made it if you hadn't kept your head and jumped,' Paul said. 'I'd never have caught him in time.'

'Then I think,' she said, becoming rapidly aware of the hurt in her leg, 'that we ought to count that one half mine.'

They all laughed and the tension was dissipated. Beatrice turned her attention to calming Varda, who was still frightened and crying, although she remained on her tightly reined pony.

Franz arrived with the runaway horse and a worried expression, and had to be told the story by an admiring Ray. Wounds were bandaged. Paul's was the deeper and more serious; hers was long, but not deep. She was even able to mount her horse with help.

Of course the hunt was over. Franz had brought along a sort of sled that he pulled behind his horse. The first carcass was already tied to this, and he added the second. Then they started back to the house, Ray in the lead this time.

Jeannie was disappointed they didn't have boar for dinner. 'Sorry,' Ray apologized, 'but it has to age before it's eaten. I promise you a real treat when it's ready, though.'

It had been quite a day. Varda had remained at such a pitch of excitement that it had finally been deemed useless to try lessons and she had been given a holiday. Beatrice and Ray were in festive moods, laughing and talking incessantly.

Only Paul seemed out of sorts. Once they had begun the trip back to the house, he had been morose and silent. He avoided Jeannie's eyes at dinner and took no part in the animated conversation.

With one part of her mind, Jeannie was glad. She had not intended to make her own feelings so obvious. More than that, her feelings for Paul were all mixed up. She was finding it harder and harder to stick to her original purpose in coming here.

Still, when she went to her own room later, she felt somewhat dispirited. That moment in Paul's arms, knowing how frightened he had been for her — it would be so wonderful to think that he loved her. She knew his type all too well, though. Concern was not love. When he loved, it would be with a concentrated and all-consuming flame, and she would have to be prepared to love him the same way. With him there were no compromises. She was not yet ready for this. There were too many doubts in her mind, too many questions unanswered.

Exhausted from the day's events, she fell asleep at once, but her sleep was uneasy. She dreamed Susan was with her and they were young girls again, happy and carefree. Max was suddenly there too. He gave Jeannie a cold look and took Susan away. Susan smiled sadly at Jeannie and went with him. Jeannie called Susan's name and tried to follow, but they began to run, until finally she lost them in a cold, wet fog.

When she saw them again they were standing on a rocky cliff, but when she got closer it was not Max, but Paul, grinning sardonically. Susan laughed, but now she was not Susan, she was Varda; and Beatrice and Ray where there too, all

119

of them laughing.

Paul left them and came to her. She sank willingly into his embrace, returning his kiss, but his kiss was as cold as the fog. She tried to resist but the blackness and fog were all about her.

She woke with a start, sitting upright in bed. The room was like ice. She must have forgotten to bank the fire — but no, it was more than that. The windows stood open, fog rolling in from the ocean, filling the room with swirling mist.

She swayed dizzily as she got up from the bed. Her leg throbbed under the bandage, much more painful than it had been before. She shook her head, sleep still clinging, and hobbled to the windows. A curtain blew over her, settling on her head as though it meant to choke her. She brushed it aside with an annoyed gesture and stepped outside.

Realization came in the same instant that the wood swayed beneath her. One foot was in the room, the other outside. She stepped back, a shiver racing the length of her spine. Had she put her full weight down on that step, she would have fallen straight through, as Susan had done, fallen to her death on the rocks.

Heart pounding, she slammed the windows closed. But, she thought, they were closed earlier, weren't they? She had checked them when she went to bed, as she always did.

Or had she? She had been so drowsy when she came in. Had she neglected to close them? She shook her head, unable to remember. Surely that must be the explanation, though, since they had been open just now, and they couldn't have opened themselves.

Unless . . . She stared hard at the windows as though they might answer the question lurking at the edge of her consciousness. Had someone come into her room and opened them, expecting her to fall . . . ?

A sound from the hall made her whirl about sharply, holding back the cry that rose in her throat. A footstep — someone was outside her door. She held her breath, staring as the knob turned. The door creaked as it opened.

Paul Langdon looked first at her bed

and then at her, holding his lamp aloft. Their eyes met. There was no romance in his gaze now.

'Have you been out?' he asked in a low voice.

'No.' Her voice sounded frightened to her own ears.

'Varda's door was open.'

She shook her head again. 'I had a bad dream,' she said, thinking she ought to explain why she was out of bed.

'Are you all right?'

'Yes, thank you. Only my fire's gone out. I was just about to build it again.'

He took his hand from the door jamb. In the wavering light she could see that his fingers were red. For the first time she looked down at herself and saw that her leg was bleeding again. Her hand was bloody as well.

He came in, closing the door softly. 'Sit down,' he said, leading her to the chair by the fire. He brought her a blanket to wrap around herself. Then, quickly and skilfully, he built a fire. When it was going well, he said, 'Wait there. I'll get fresh bandages for your leg.'

He was back in a few minutes with water and the bandages. Kneeling before her, he removed the old cloth, tossing that into the fire, and cleaned and bandaged the cut expertly. His hands were amazingly gentle. They said nothing to one another during this time.

When he was finished, he stood again. 'You'll be all right?' he asked.

She had meant to tell him she was frightened — but how could she, when he was part of what frightened her?

'Yes,' she said, unable now to meet his eyes.

'Good night, then.' Either he did not notice her change of attitude or he chose to ignore it.

She climbed back into bed when he was gone. She could not decide if he had come to her room because he thought she had left Varda's door open, or because he was concerned about her and wanted to assure himself that she was all right.

After a few minutes she stole from her bed again and crossed the room to bolt her door securely.

9

It was one of those days that drop broad hints of spring. The water looked too blue to belong to the Atlantic and the reflections of sunlight were dazzling.

'Easy,' Ray said, putting out his hand to help Jeannie into the launch. Despite a week of healing, her leg was still tender. She moved gingerly to the seat and in a minute they were running out into the water.

It seemed strange to be off the island. She had been here nearly three weeks and in one sense the time seemed all too short. In another sense, however, she felt as if she had always been here. It was her other life, before she had come here, that seemed foreign to her now. She thought of what it would be like in New York City just at the moment — rivers of cars on the streets, horns honking, throngs of people.

As if aware of her train of thought, Ray said, 'I guess you've missed the hustle and bustle of the big city.'

'It's funny, but I really haven't,' she said. 'To think that less than a month ago I was at The Sherry.'

An eyebrow went up. 'The Sherry, Netherlands? You live well for a working girl,' he said.

She realized her mistake at once. 'I like to pamper myself occasionally,' she said, and, before he could pursue the subject, 'But I had you picked out as the one for bright lights and city life. I was sure you were bored to tears on the island.'

'Sometimes I am. When the finances were a little better, I used to take off for the city once or twice a month. I still could, I guess, in the yacht, but it takes money to operate that, and Paul would never approve. Anyway, to tell you the truth, I've been enjoying the island more of late.' He said the last with a wink.

She smiled back at him, fully aware that his flirtations weren't serious. She was glad he had been there to dispel a bit of the gloom. The past few days had been peculiar ones. Beatrice had been friendly and cheerful, and Varda was a delightful child.

Paul remained as unfathomable as ever. She had the impression he never ceased watching her — so often she looked up to find his eyes on her — but she didn't know whether to be flattered or intimidated by his attention.

The relationship between father and child remained a puzzle. She was certain he genuinely loved his daughter and Varda seemed equally devoted to her father. Although the child had Susan's face, it was clear she was her father's child. Jeannie had no difficulty imagining her grown, reigning over the Purlieu with the disdain for ordinary mortals that seemed inherent to the Langdons. But the mysteries remained, not the least of them that locked bedroom door, and the nights Paul spent sleeping on the floor of his daughter's bedroom.

'Land ho,' Ray said, interrupting her thoughts. In the distance she could see the coast and as they came nearer, the houses of the Landing. They looked less dismal and ominous than when she had seen them last.

She could see that she and Ray were

the center of attention as the launch pulled up to the landing. People on the dock stopped what they were doing to stare and others came to their windows. She waited for him to help her out of the boat.

'What are you going to do with yourself?' she asked. Her plans, as announced earlier, consisted mostly of shopping. There were other things she wanted to do but she hadn't mentioned those to the Langdons.

'Oh, I've got plenty of errands of my own.' He looked at his watch. 'It's one now. Suppose we meet back here at four? That'll get us back before dark.'

When he had gone, she went in search of a public telephone. She found one at a service station. There was only one M.D. listed in town, a Doctor Morris. He was out when she called but the woman who answered gave her an appointment for three thirty.

Her next stop was the coffee shop she had been in before. Luck was with her: the same helpful waitress was behind the counter and there was only one other customer, a pink-cheeked lady who was preparing to leave when Jeannie sat down.

When she had a cup of coffee set before her and she and the waitress were alone, Jeannie said, 'I want to thank you again for helping me the last time I was here.'

The waitress's smile was a trifle uncertain. 'You're the one who was looking for a way to the Purlieu, aren't you?' she asked.

'Yes, and I got it, thanks to you.'

The woman went to the end of the counter and busied herself briefly with washing cups, after which she poured herself a cup of coffee. Jeannie waited patiently, sure a naturally inquisitive nature would come to the fore.

'You been out there all this time?' the waitress asked finally.

Jeannie nodded. 'Yes. It's quite a lovely place, really.'

The waitress drank her coffee and picked at a broken fingernail. 'Now where? New York, I suppose.'

Jeannie looked surprised. 'Oh, no, I'm going back to the island. I'm working there.'

'Oh?' She resorted to chewing on the nail.

'I don't know why,' Jeannie said with a laugh, 'but I was actually afraid of going there. It seemed so spooky. And when all the men here refused to take me over, well, I don't know what I expected. That it was haunted, or something. Say,' she said as if the question had just occurred to her, 'why wouldn't they, anyway? Take me across, I mean?'

The woman cast a nervous glance toward the door. 'I don't know,' she said. 'The local people don't take too kindly to the place.'

'There's one local girl who comes over a couple of times a week to help with the housework.'

'That's Joyce Ann Weathers. She's got to. They need the money bad, or I don't expect she'd go either. No one else will anymore.'

Jeannie grew sober. 'I hope you aren't trying to tell me there's anything seriously wrong on the island.'

'I couldn't say,' the waitress replied with a shrug. 'I've never been one to gossip.'

Jeannie turned on her stool to face the

woman directly. 'But if I'm in any kind of danger or anything . . . '

The woman set her cup down and gave her a hard look. 'Listen,' she said in a lower voice, 'if you want to know what I think, you'll get back on the same bus that brought you here and be on your way. That's my advice.'

'But why? What's wrong with the place?'

'I don't know. No one does. Not exactly, at least. But there's something funny going on, that's for sure. You and Joyce Ann, you're the only ones to come back from there.'

'Come back? What do you mean?'

'I mean just that.' She came to where Jeannie sat and leaned down, her arms on the counter. 'There's been four different girls go over there to work. Two of them from the town here and two who were strangers. The first one from town, Liz Cotter, she just disappeared into thin air. When her family didn't hear from her for a few weeks, they sent over to ask about her. They got a note back saying she wasn't there and hadn't been for a month. They said they thought she had just up and come home, but no one here saw her.'

'Maybe she just ran away,' Jeannie suggested.

'Not unless she flapped her wings and flew away. She'd have to come by boat to the landing here and no one ever saw her get out of a boat.'

'What about the others?' Jeannie's coffee was cold but she did not want to break the woman's train of thought, now that she was talking.

'Mary Witten went over to work a while after that.'

'And she never came back either?'

'Well, I guess you could say she did, in a sense,' the woman said with a dry laugh. 'They found her washed up on the rocks in a dinghy, a spot about five miles down the coast. It looked like she'd tried to leave in that little boat and didn't make it.'

'How awful,' Jeannie said. 'And the others?'

The waitress shrugged her shoulders. 'They weren't from around here, so no one here knows exactly what happened. But they were seen going over there and they were never seen coming back.'

Jeannie stared down into her coffee cup. Susan had not been able to leave the island either. *But that's ridiculous*, she told herself. *I've come back and no one tried to prevent me from leaving.*

Of course, she was expected to return to Langdon's Purlieu.

She fumbled in her purse for money to pay her tab, and pushed it across the counter. Time was getting short. 'Thank you for the warning,' she said, standing.

'You're going back?'

Jeannie nodded. 'But I'll be careful,' she said. Her informant looked dubious.

Jeannie had shopping to do, not only because she really did want and need certain things but because this was her excuse for the trip to town. By the time she had made all of her purchases, sending the larger items directly to the landing, it was nearly three thirty, and time for her appointment with the doctor.

★ ★ ★

In a red suit and white beard, Doctor Morris would have made a perfect Santa. He had an intelligent face, though, and she guessed he would be a difficult man to deceive. His eyes went at once to the bandage on her leg and, assuming that to be the reason for her visit, he suggested right off that he take a look at it.

'I'm not here about the leg,' she told him frankly. 'Although I suppose it might be a good idea if you looked at it while I'm here. Actually I just wanted to talk to you.'

'I see.' He indicated a chair. 'Well, why don't you have a seat there and you can talk while I'm examining this.'

She sat down and he took a small stool in front of her and began to unwind the bandages.

'Whoever did this knew what they were doing,' he said.

'Mr. Langdon,' she said. He nodded without comment.

'I'm actually here to ask about another patient of yours,' she said. 'Mrs. Langdon — Susan Langdon, that is. I believe she came to you for treatment.'

His hands had stopped. He looked up at her, his expression grave. 'I'm sure you must realize that professional ethics prevent my discussing another patient with you.'

'I think the circumstances warrant it,' she replied. 'I'm Mrs. Langdon's sister. Half-sister, actually. I'm staying at the Purlieu just now, although . . . ' She hesitated but she knew it would have to be said. ' . . . they don't know who I am. I'm there as an employee.'

'I see.' He returned to examining the cut on her leg, but his hands worked automatically and she knew he was thinking over what she had said.

'What exactly is it you want to know? Careful, this will sting a bit.'

She winced as he probed the cut. 'How my sister died,' she said.

'There was a gentleman here, too, asking about her death,' he said.

'Lou Benner, our family attorney, and a good friend besides. I've talked to him already.'

'Then you must know what I told him.'

'Yes, but I wasn't convinced. I wanted

to hear from you.'

He sighed and went to get fresh bandages and antiseptic. 'Very simply, Mrs. Langdon died from injuries she suffered from a fall. If you know the house, then you know there is nothing particularly mysterious about such an accident.'

'But is there any possibility . . . ?'

He shook his head firmly. 'That she was pushed? None whatsoever. You might as well know, your sister was not a well woman.' He held up a hand to forestall her response. 'No, there's nothing especially mysterious about that either. How long has it been since you had seen your sister?'

She looked down, embarrassed. 'A number of years,' she said quietly. 'Since before she married Mr. Langdon.'

He was thoughtful for a moment. Probably, she thought, he was seeking the most tactful way to approach the subject. He seated himself again and began to administer to her leg. 'There's hardly any need for me to tell you what you must already know about her. Hers was not a strong character. From my conversations with her I had an impression she was very much dominated by her late father, a man of strong will.'

'Yes, she was.'

'Well, then, you know how she was. When he died she was left more or less without an anchor. She attached herself to Paul Langdon as something of a father substitute.'

He looked up at her and she nodded. 'Yes, I think you're entirely right.'

'It wasn't a very satisfactory arrangement, in my opinion,' he said, 'but that's only guesswork, and really that part of it was none of my business. People marry for all sorts of reasons.'

'Sometimes love is the least of it, it seems to me,' Jeannie said.

He looked up at her and nodded again. 'Exactly. Anyway, I think he must have been flattered at first, and there's no denying she was a beautiful woman. However, if I may be frank, she was also a neurotic one. For some time she had been addicted to sleeping pills. That was already true when she first came to me.

She must have been taking them since she was quite young.' He looked at her again for confirmation.

'I never knew, but it seems likely now that I think back. She was always a problem sleeper, even as a child.'

'Yes. Well . . . ' He had finished with the bandage and stood up. 'Those things are self-defeating over time, as you probably know. The body builds up a tolerance to them, so that you need stronger and stronger doses. I tried to persuade her to let me put her in a clinic where she could be gradually weaned off them, but she wouldn't hear of it. There was nothing for me to do but prescribe more and more pills for her.'

He had gone to the window, but when he turned back to her she saw that his expression was one of grief, and she realized with a shock that he too carried a burden of guilt for Susan's death.

'In a way,' he said, 'I suppose I'm in part at fault, but a doctor learns to shuck off that sort of blame — or at least he should, else he'd quickly go crazy. At any rate, this is how your sister came to have her accident. Something woke her during the night. No one knows what, exactly. It might have been nothing more than a bad dream. She was heavily drugged. She got up and for some reason went to her window. She fell from an unsafe balcony and died in the fall.'

'Mr. Benner said there was a cut,' she said, but without much hope.

'Yes, at her throat. Hard to say what it was.'

'Might it have been a bite mark?'

He thought briefly. 'It was more the sort of thing she might have gotten if she was trimming her hair, which I understand she did with a straight razor, and her hand slipped. But it doesn't really matter, it was much too slight to have caused her death. She had lost some blood, apparently, but not enough to have made her ill.'

'Might she have been struck, or have struggled, and wouldn't the fall have camouflaged any bruises?'

He looked dubious. 'It's possible, but I rather doubt it.'

She sighed and looked at her watch. It

was nearly time to meet Ray. She stood up.

'I'm sorry I haven't been more helpful,' the doctor said, 'but as I explained at the beginning, there was nothing particularly mysterious about her death.'

'Only that wound. I'd still like to know more about that.'

He smiled tolerantly but in a way to show he thought she was being foolish. 'I can assure you,' he said, 'it was of no importance. Unless,' he laughed to show he was making a joke, 'you think she was the victim of a vampire.'

A warning bell sounded somewhere far back in her mind. Something someone had said, but who . . . ? It came back to her suddenly. 'What a strange coincidence,' she said aloud. 'Lou Benner mentioned that subject in connection with the Langdons; something to do with the family history.'

Doctor Morris assumed a stern look. 'I was only making a joke, miss. It would be tragic if you were to let your imagination run away with you, which I fear you may be in danger of doing. Your sister's death was the result of an accidental fall. I would stake my professional reputation on it.'

'I'm sorry,' she said, giving him her hand. 'You're right, I'm being too imaginative. Thank you for all your help. There is one more favor I'd like to ask of you. What I told you, about being Mrs. Langdon's sister and at the Purlieu as an employee, was said in confidence.'

'I won't pretend to approve of any of this,' he said, 'but I shall respect that confidence.'

'Thank you,' she said again, but at the door another thought occurred to her. 'Doctor, if Susan were so heavily drugged the night of her death, wouldn't it have taken something rather major to have awakened her?'

'Perhaps. If she had taken a very heavy dose, yes, it would. But perhaps she was only mildly sedated at the time, so that a slight noise or even a bad dream might wake her.'

'But if she had taken only a small dose and could be so easily awakened, how could she have staggered so unknowingly onto the balcony?'

She saw from his frown that the question had not occurred to him before. It was four o'clock, however, and she had no time now to pursue the subject further. 'Good day, Doctor,' she said, and let herself out.

A flower-bordered walk led her alongside the house and thus to the sidewalk. There she turned, and nearly collided with Ray Langdon.

'Well, I'll be . . . ' he said. 'I was running late and hurrying to get to the boat. I figured you'd be waiting in a pique of temper.' He looked at Doctor Morris's shingle. 'But what are you doing here? You're not sick, are you?'

She wondered if she looked as guilty as she felt. 'No, I thought I'd have my leg checked while I was in town,' she said. 'But what are you doing here?'

'Oh, I'm just finishing up some errands of my own,' he said, his face innocent. 'Come on, we may as well walk back together — unless you've got some more things to do?'

'No, I'm quite finished.' They fell into step together.

'You needn't have worried,' he said. 'About your leg, I mean. Paul's as good as a doctor.'

'Doctor Morris seemed to think so.'

She looked around and, as though simply admiring the town, looked behind them. With the exception of the doctor's office, the street was a residential one, a narrow back street off the main thoroughfare, with nothing on the surface to recommend it to Ray.

She had the feeling that he was there because he had been following her.

10

Jeannie's packages were waiting at the boat. Most of them were readily identifiable — hanging bags from the dress shop where she had supplemented her meager wardrobe, boxes and bags from the toy shop and dime store that would keep Varda delighted for weeks to come. One tall, flat box caught Ray's attention before they even reached the launch.

'What's that?' he asked. 'Looks like a table without legs.'

'It's a mirror. It's just too difficult to get by with only the one out of my purse and Maria just hasn't managed to find one for me no matter how many times I've asked.'

He gave her a sideways look that she thought was anxious, but almost at once he laughed. 'I hadn't thought what a nuisance it must be for you, but it only confirms my theory that beauty like yours requires little attention.'

'It requires enough that I need a mirror,' she said.

'Let me make a suggestion. When we get back, why don't you let me take this on up to your room without making any mention of it to anyone else?'

'Ray . . . ' She paused in the act of handing him a dress bag. 'Why aren't there any mirrors in the house?' She had asked this question before, of Maria, but had gotten no answer.

'Mama has a fetish about them,' he said without hesitation. 'She thinks if she doesn't have to watch the process, she won't grow old. I do have one in my room, you know. We all do, in fact. Paul, Varda, Maria. I don't know why Maria didn't mention the fact that your room doesn't; I'd have seen that you got one.'

She said nothing. When the loading was done, he helped her into the launch and a few minutes later they were headed for the island.

She had a great many things on her mind and she turned some of them over as they went. For one thing, Ray had lied to her about the mirrors. She knew that neither Varda's room nor Beatrice's had any mirrors unless they were well concealed. But why should he lie about something like that? What possible significance could mirrors have, that the Langdons avoided them so?

Her thoughts soon turned back to Susan's death, and she went over again her conversation with Doctor Morris, and the question of Susan's sedation on that fateful night. If Susan had been awakened easily, then she was not as much under the influence of drugs as everyone supposed. And if not, how had she managed to go out onto a balcony that she undeniably knew was unsafe?

What had awakened Susan, anyway? She herself had recently been awakened during the night, by what she did not know, and she had found the windows open; had nearly fallen to her own death. Had that near-accident been staged? And might not Susan's accident have been managed in a similar manner? That only brought her back, however, to the critical questions — by whom, and why?

She found herself remembering her

conversation with the waitress at the coffee shop. What had happened to those young women who had come to work at the Purlieu? Or was a natural resentment against the aristocracy merely taking advantage of unfortunate coincidence? One girl might have run away without informing her family, after all, and another might have drowned accidentally, without either signifying anything sinister on the part of the Langdons. As for the other two, they might have left the island without being noticed by the townspeople.

Not likely, another little voice in her head said. The people of Grandy's Landing gave every indication of being observant, especially where the Langdons were concerned.

Vampires? She dismissed that idea as ridiculous. Doctor Morris had been right, there; she was letting her imagination run rampant.

'You're very quiet,' Ray said, breaking into her train of thought.

'Just thinking,' she said. 'Tell me, why don't the local people want to work at the island?'

'Oh ho,' he said, grinning, 'the townsfolk have been entertaining you with dark tales of the Langdons, have they? All right, my love, let's have it — what did they say about us this time? Are we cooking young maidens for our holiday feasts, or am I Count Cagliostro, kept alive by black magic?'

She laughed because without knowing it he was poking fun at her own dark imaginings. 'Neither, but they aren't exactly wild about coming for visits.'

He dismissed that with a toss of his head. 'They've never been encouraged to be friendly,' he said.

She did not mean to give up so easily. 'But there must be more to it than that.'

He gave her a searching look. 'You've been talking to Louise Donald.'

'I may have. Who is she?'

'The waitress in that little coffee shop you visited.' He smiled at her consternation. 'It's a small town and I was only across the street. I couldn't help seeing you in there chatting with her, and I know the kind of tales she likes to tell. You heard about missing maidens, am I right?'

'You're right,' she admitted sheepishly.

'Well, if it will make you feel better,' he said, directing his attention to bringing the launch around to the landing, 'one of the village girls who worked for us ran away. We couldn't tell her family but her mother was almost certain the girl had a sweetheart she was meeting somewhere. She got a letter the day before she disappeared. Mother and Franz both confirmed that. We just supposed it was from the boyfriend, making arrangements to meet somewhere. So much for that mystery.

'Then, to confound things, another girl who was working over here was drowned in a boating accident. I believe you were warned about dangerous tides. Well, she was warned too, but apparently she thought she knew them better than we did. She decided to try to come into town on her own in the dinghy, which was foolish — that little thing was never intended for ocean boating. It came apart and she drowned. So of course those two incidents coming close together like that gave rise to all sorts of ominous stories about us.'

The boat bumped against the landing.

He got out and tied the launch up before giving her a hand.

'What about the other two?' she asked.

'Whew,' he said, eyebrows lifting. 'You got the whole works, didn't you? Well, there's nothing very dramatic about those two. They both just left us. Seems they didn't care much for life over here. Many people don't, especially sweet young ladies. I'm surprised you've stayed so long. I wonder what the attraction is?'

'Maybe it's your winning charm,' she suggested, smiling as she took one of the parcels from him.

He did not smile back. 'No,' he said, 'not my charm, I think.'

★　★　★

Evenings were generally quiet at the house. Beatrice Langdon had provided Jeannie with some embroidery work with which she sometimes busied herself. More often she read. The library held several hundred volumes, ranging from classic works of fiction to reference works, so she was always able to find something of interest.

The evening after her visit to town she decided to look in the library for something to read. She walked idly along the wall of books, scanning titles, but nothing really caught her fancy. She glanced upward, wondering about the shelves that were not only out of reach but beyond her range of vision. A set of library steps on wheels stood in one corner. She mounted them to take a closer look at the upper shelves.

The word 'vampire' almost seemed to jump out at her. She removed the book that had caught her eye — *Varney the Vampire; or, a Feast of Blood*. One of the penny-dreadful novels of the last century. Written, the title page told her, by one Thomas Prest in 1847. She smiled and closed the book, putting it back on the shelf.

Beside it was *Dracula*, by Irish author Bram Stoker. She did not have to remove it from the shelf to know that it too dealt with a vampire. She had seen the movie adaptation long ago. Next to that book was *The Vampire, His Kith and Kin*, by Montague Summers.

She ran her eyes along the shelf, and the shelf above that. The entire section was devoted to the subject of vampires.

For a long time she remained on the ladder, her eyes moving back and forth along the rows of books. Finally, she began to select from among them. When she had as many as she felt she could safely carry, she took them to her bedroom, where she carefully bolted her door and checked to see that the windows were securely closed. She took time to build up her fire, and sat in front of it with the books on the floor beside her.

She turned to *Dracula* first, because she was vaguely familiar with the fictional tale. The author painted a vivid and chilling portrait of his monster, who dwelt in a Transylvanian castle. She could almost see him through the eyes of the book's protagonist.

'Within stood a tall, old man, clean-shaven save for a long white moustache, and clad in black from head to foot, without a single speck of colour about him anywhere . . . He moved impulsively forward and holding out his hand, grasped mine with a strength that made me wince, an effect which was not lessened by the fact that it seemed as cold as ice — more like the hand of a dead than a living man . . . His face was a strong — very strong — aquiline, with high bridge of the thin nose and peculiarly arched nostrils; with lofty domed forehead and hair growing scantily about the temples, but profusely elsewhere. His eyebrows were very massive, almost meeting over the nose . . . the mouth . . . was fixed and rather cruel-looking, with peculiarly sharp white teeth; these protruded over the lips, whose remarkable ruddiness showed astonishing vitality in a man of his years. For the rest, his ears were pale and at the tops extremely pointed; the chin was broad and strong, and the cheeks firm though thin. The general effect was one of extraordinary pallor . . . I could not but notice that his hands were rather coarse — broad with squat fingers. Strange to say there were hairs in the centre of the palm. The nails were long and fine, and cut to a sharp point . . . the Count's eyes gleamed . . . '

The Count, she read, skimming through

the book, was four hundred years old. He kept a wolf-pack at his command and he had the power of metamorphosis, or physical change into other forms — not, as she had supposed, merely a bat, but a wolf as well, or he could become a mere cloud of mist, or even of glittering dust. He lived to consume blood, the vitalizing life-giving fluid.

Appropriately grim, she thought, for an old gothic novel, but obviously the work of a vivid imagination. She laid the book aside and took up the Montague Summers volume.

' . . . It partakes of the dark natures and possesses the mysterious and terrible qualities . . . yet the vampire is not strictly a demon . . . ' Summers had written in 1928, later than Stoker, but she could not tell how much of his material was factually reliable and how much pure fiction.

She was surprised at some of the names in her collection. The vampire subject had appealed to some notables. Goethe was here in *The Bride of Corinth*, and Scott with his translation of Burgher's ballad

Leonore. Southey contributed *Thalaba* and Lord Byron *The Vampyre.* A book of collected words revealed a poem by Gautier, *La Morte Amoreuse,* short stories by M. R. James and E. F. Benson, and excerpts from Baudelaire, de Sade and Le Fanu.

The vampire first came into existence ' . . . through the coming together of the Devil, which was in his primeval form, the serpent, that is the viper or adder, and a vile Witch, she also like the serpent in her evil,' according to Le Fanu.

Byron wrote, 'But first, on earth as vampire sent, Thy corpse shall from its tomb be rent: Then ghastly haunt thy native place . . . '

It seemed that the vampire was as old as mankind. He dated back to the literature of Ovid, and she was reminded that Odysseus, in his legends, had to give blood to the shades of the underworld. It was in the sixteen hundreds, however, that the legends began to abound and vampires proliferated. They were most common, apparently, in the Balkan regions — Hungary, Albania, Poland,

Silesia, Moravia . . .

She looked up from her readings and stared into the fire. Were the Langdons from the Balkans? She had heard mention of that region, hadn't she? But surely their name was English?

She went back to her reading. The ways of detecting vampires, she learned, ranged from harelips to red hair. There were methods, too, for finding the vampire's resting place. In one of them, a young boy pure in body and spirit rode a black stallion through a graveyard. Whatever grave the horse refused to cross over, therein would be found a vampire.

Protection against vampires likewise varied greatly, ranging from wreaths of garlic to the crucifix. Hawthorn branches and whitethorn were effective, it was believed, and holy water.

One item in particular caught her attention. The vampire was said to hate mirrors and never had them in his house. Some authorities said it was because he had no reflection; others believed that the reflection, representing the soul, might be imprisoned in the glass.

She closed the last of the books and sat looking into her fire. The wind rattled the shutters and she felt cold, despite the blaze before her. She dressed for bed and, once again checking the bolt at her door, retired; but she did not sleep easily. She started up every time the wind rattled the shutters at her windows, as if someone were trying to gain entrance.

11

Jeannie woke in the morning after a restless night and with a sense of dread. The house seemed bleaker and darker than ever, and when she threw open the windows it was upon a dismal gray day.

After lessons and lunch, she took a book of verse and went out into the courtyard by herself. The sun had managed to dispel most of the fog and she thought that the out-of-doors and some light verse might dispel her gloom.

She found her attention constantly wandering from the book. Finally she slammed it closed in frustration and, dropping it into the pocket of her coat, left the courtyard for the path beyond the house. She took the one that led toward the beach, but went only as far as the cliff, remembering the warnings about dangerous tides.

A fragile spring had come timidly. The greens of the grass and trees were still pale and blended with browns, and the air remained cold and brisk. Still, there was an unmistakable lift to it, a scent of blooming things and fresh growth that would not be denied.

A twig snapped behind her. She turned quickly to see Paul approaching her. He did not have the air of a man just out for a stroll. She remembered his order that she was not to go out alone, and she thought he might be angry with her, but although his expression was sober it was not angry. She waited silently for him to join her.

'The view from the point up there is quite spectacular,' he said as he came up. She said nothing but let him lead her to the spot he meant. The view was indeed spectacular. The island lay spread out at her feet, and off to the side was the ocean lashing against the cliffs.

'On a good day you can see the mainland,' he said, pointing in that general direction, but this day she saw only ocean.

She was surprised to see how his features were softened. He looked younger and she knew his soul caressed this place and the view the way a lover caresses his beloved. She turned away before he saw her look at what she knew instinctively were private feelings.

'You've taken up some peculiar reading,' he said after a moment.

She gave him a surprised look. 'Have you been searching my room?' she asked.

He grinned and shook his head. 'That would hardly be necessary. You left a rather conspicuous gap on the shelves. It was not hard to make out what subject had captured your fancy.'

'I thought it rather peculiar that your library should have such an extensive collection of volumes on what is, let us agree, a rather odd subject,' she said frankly, meeting his gaze.

He studied her for a long moment as though weighing something in his mind. Then he said, 'No, of course not; you aren't the easily frightened sort. Come here.' He took her by the elbow, but gently, and brought her to a huge boulder nearby, putting his own coat over the rock for her to sit on. The wind whipped the scarf around his neck and ruffled his hair, but he seemed not to mind.

'I said when you first came here that we weren't ordinary people,' he said, shoving his hands deep into the pockets of his trousers. 'The Langdons didn't always live isolated on this little island, you know. At one time we had houses and estates in nearly a dozen countries. My great-great-grandfather's family has a history that goes back further than the England that claims them. His wife was Moravian. If I showed you a map of the lands she inherited you'd think she owned all the Balkans — and she did, nearly.'

He paused and, thinking she ought to say something, Jeannie commented, 'You lost a great deal of money.'

He laughed drily. 'Yes, we did do that. I'm trying to sell a property in London and one in Nova Scotia. That will just about leave this place clear and allow us to live out the rest of our lives here, if we economize.'

'But surely the money you got . . . ' She caught herself, blushing furiously as she realized her mistake. She finished lamely,

'I understood your former wife was well-to-do.'

He gave her a hard look. 'Not wealthy enough, as it turned out.' He looked away from her, out over the fog-clouded ocean. 'The money was only a part of our problem,' he said. 'You wanted to know why I have so many books on vampirism? It's because I thought it behooved me to know as much as possible about a subject that haunts our family. You see, Miss Burke, they run in the family, vampires do.'

She gasped and her mouth fell open, but she could think of nothing to say.

'Does that frighten you after all?' he asked, looking back at her again.

Some sixth sense told her that the answer was vitally important. 'No,' she managed to say, 'only . . . you must be joking, surely?'

He shook his head sadly. 'That was no joke.'

'But I thought vampires were a myth, relegated to the Middle Ages.'

'There was a famous trial in Germany after the First World War, and another in

Britain in 1949, in which it was decided that the accused were vampires. And in 1952 in Italy authorities exhumed the body of a woman who had died more than thirty years before. According to the reports, she was perfectly preserved and bled profusely when wounded.'

Her expression made him smile again. 'Yes, I can see you are shocked. I tell you these things, however, only to rid you of your disbelief. The thing in which to disbelieve is not vampires. By whatever name you choose to call them, they do and have existed. But the issue has been clouded by myth and superstition and error. Once one is able to lay aside one's fear and study the subject openly, the facts seem less shocking.'

'As is often the case,' she said.

'Exactly.' He paused, seeming to sort out his thoughts, and put one foot up on the rock beside her. He might have been a college professor delivering a well-rehearsed lecture. It occurred to her that perhaps this was somewhat the case; perhaps he had rehearsed it for the time when he would tell it to her.

'What we call the vampire was the *voordalak* in Slavonic, the *wampyr* in Magyar. Of course the association with bats is recent. When travellers began to bring back accounts of South American bats that drank blood, the connection was too good to pass up. Before that, though, the vampire was associated with a variety of creatures, especially the owl.

'By whatever name, the vampire didn't come into his own in Europe until the seventeenth century — a time, of course, when superstition and legend were rampant. Just as there were witch crazes, so too there were vampire crazes, and a lot of silly tales were made up to support the charges that were brought against those accused of being vampires.'

'As with those accused of being witches,' she said.

'Yes, it was much the same. The subject was doomed to be surrounded by gibberish, simply because of the beliefs and fears of the times. So the vampire was alternately said to be a demon with the power to enter a dead body, or the spirit of the person who died, for one reason or another condemned to wander the earth as a creature of the night. Either one fitted in nicely with the general nonsense of the day — All Saints' Day, Samhain, All Souls' Day. There was a plethora of rituals concerned with the dead roaming the earth.'

'Even today many people take the ideas of ghosts seriously.'

'All of this, however, was just the way those people had of explaining a phenomenon they couldn't understand. But just because we can discard most of those old beliefs doesn't mean we can discard the vampire as a reality. They'd have had no need to invent explanations for the vampire if he didn't exist — bear that in mind.'

A ferocious gust of wind swept over them, as though the island spirits resented his sharing these confidences with her. She hugged her coat closer and wondered that he didn't seem to notice the weather.

'All right, then,' she asked, 'how do you explain them?'

'By digging down to the substratum of

fact. To begin with, a great many reported cases of vampirism probably weren't vampirism at all. Often the real problem was premature burial, or the burial of someone in a state of suspended animation or catalepsy.'

'*The House of Usher*,' she said.

'Yes. Poe mostly likely based his tale on some real incident. There were a number of reported cases of this early in this century, and in earlier days, before routine embalming and before medical science had made it possible to determine for certain that someone really was dead, it must have happened even more often. Sometimes the person didn't even get buried; he would revive on the way to the ceremony. Which wasn't necessarily a happy circumstance for him, because he was then certain to be looked upon as a vampire.

'And most likely a lot of stories sprang from the most common affliction, human malice. The church wielded her influence, too. A wrongdoer, for instance, or an excommunicate, was threatened with returning as a vampire. And there were always tightly knit groups in every town, the kind of people hostile to anything unusual. An old, poor woman might be called a witch; a deformed person or one with a harelip could become a vampire. In certain times and places, all you needed to be labelled a vampire was a pair of blue eyes.'

She could not help thinking what might have happened to someone like himself, with eyes of silver.

'Then we had the plague, with its mysterious death and its stench. The plague and the vampire epidemic are coincidental in time. Look at the symptoms of the plague — exhaustion, faintness as though from a great loss of blood — and no matter what the local so-called doctor could do, the person died soon afterward. Sounds exactly like what Mister Stoker wrote, doesn't it?'

'Yes, but these are explanations of mistaken belief in vampires. You said that vampires really did exist.'

He nodded, pleased with her openness to his explanation. 'Yes, they did. Because along with all this, there were forms of psychosis, mental aberrations, call them what you will. Probably many of them sprang up after the fact.'

'After every crime, there are always a few crackpots confessing falsely,' she said. 'I'll bet a lot of it was the same sort of thing. Vampires were fashionable, so to speak, so a few misguided souls began confessing to being vampires.'

'No doubt there was a lot of that, but there truly are people with insane cravings for blood; that's documented in present-day psychiatry. And there are mental diseases concerning the dead that parallel vampirism closely enough. Necrophilia, necrophagia, plenty of big words. Vampirism itself, strangely enough, has rarely been renamed by the experts. It's still vampirism, or pseudovampirism, or less often hemothymia. It's a form of paranoia, as I understand it. In its milder forms, the victim imagines himself as a vampire, perhaps dreaming of such experiences. In its more extreme forms he may go further. He may commit acts that . . . well, that parallel the acts of a vampire. Drinking blood, for example.

And some people are biters; they bite their partners hard enough to draw blood, which they lick from the wounds.'

He hesitated, searching for words. 'There was a family member way back, an aunt many times removed, who was executed as a vampire. God only knows what her crime actually was. Maybe she just happened to like to chase butterflies. Anyway, they ran a stake through her heart.'

She dared not tell him she had heard this story already.

'Bear in mind,' he went on, 'our family was rich, lords of the castle. If you know anything at all about people, you can imagine that they were resented and hated for being rich in a land that was poor. Vampirism gave legitimacy to that hatred, and the charge stuck. It tainted the entire family. A cousin killed himself from shame, and that only made things worse. Suicides, you see, were sure-fire bets to come back as vampires. Within a generation, the family was generally regarded as a breed of vampires.'

'How cruel,' she said, imagining what

an awful curse this must have been in earlier times.

He smiled gratefully. 'It was, but the family of course was arrogant, and for the most part untouchable. They withdrew, living more and more within the confines of their own estates. Some branches migrated to new countries. That's how we came to be here. And there was a good bit of inner marriage. That was another tragic mistake founded on ignorance. It produced some insanity. Not rampant, thank God, but enough to make matters worse. One poor old uncle, finally convinced of the legends, decided he must be a vampire and went after a couple of local villagers. That resulted in his manor house being burned to the ground. Needless to say, he died in the fire.'

He sighed sadly. 'Of course, by the time we came here, there was hardly any family left and the vampire craze was over, but the old tales lingered on, especially within the family. Which brings us to my father. Which is really what I started out to tell you.'

'Only if you feel that you must.'

He met her eyes frankly. 'I think it's necessary.' He looked away, and after a moment resumed his story. 'His chief fault was that he was just a little weak-minded, and following in the footsteps of a father, my grandfather, who was exceptionally astute. Neither my father nor his brother were suited to filling those shoes. Everything went wrong, till it began to seem to my father that he was accursed. Then his brother was killed. Later we found out that it was an accident, but at the time it looked like suicide. My father accepted it as such, and it was more or less the final straw.

'He gave himself up to drinking and drugs; but worst of all, somehow he accepted the old family curse as applying to him. In some dark corner of his mind, he began to believe that he was a vampire.

'That's why we had to isolate ourselves here, you see. And how our fortunes sank so low. My mother did what she could, but she had no experience or training to cope with running estates and she had a sick husband on her hands, not to mention two small children. Everything

170

simply went bad. Lands were sold or mortgaged, even given away, until there was virtually nothing left by the time my father died.'

He had come to the end of his story, it seemed. He was thoughtful for several minutes and Jeannie respected his silence, looking out over the water.

'I'm sorry,' he said finally, 'it's a gloomy story but I wanted you to hear it.'

'But it's all history,' she said, jumping up from the rock where she sat. 'It's all over. Why let it direct your life now?'

'Is it really over?' he asked bitterly. 'My family has been cursed by these stories. How do I know that it's ended? When will it strike again? What's to say that it isn't in my blood, to be passed on to my descendants?'

He spoke with such unexpected fervor that she was startled. 'But that's impossible,' she said, grabbing his arm impulsively. 'Little Varda couldn't be sweeter, or more . . . more . . . '

She meant to say 'more normal,' but the words wouldn't come. Because she knew in her heart that it wasn't true.

Varda wasn't normal, her life here wasn't normal, and how did she know which had come first, the chicken or the egg? She remembered the bolt on Varda's door, and his orders that she was not to be alone with the child.

She knew from his eyes that he was following all these thoughts as they raced through her mind. 'Oh, it can't be,' she cried. 'You've let all this gloom and these dark legends influence you too much. Varda's different from other children, of course she is, but it's because she's lived differently. She's anything but psychotic. And this sort of thing couldn't be inherited.'

'Couldn't it? How do we know?' He looked desperate. He was begging her to clear away the confusion in his mind and she groped for the right words to help him.

'But . . . but she's never done any of those things . . . '

A look of horror came across his face. He was remembering something, she thought — something particularly awful. It sent him reeling away from her and then, almost before she knew what had happened, he was gone, racing away down the path, and she was left with her own grim thoughts.

She stood for a moment looking after him. Her impulse was to run to him and try to comfort him, but she knew he was not that type man. When he wanted or needed her he would come to her. Later, no doubt, he would be embarrassed that he had let her see as much of his inner feeling as he had just now, but she was grateful for the urge that had caused him to do so.

He had gone without his coat. She took it from the rock and hurried back toward the house. The air seemed to have turned colder.

12

The door to Paul's den was closed when Jeannie came in. She hesitated a moment, wanting to go to him, but in the end she left his coat on a hook in the entryway and went to her own room without seeing him.

She continued to puzzle over what he had told her. The nagging truth was that he hadn't quite told her everything. He had stopped short of the truth about the present and the people now on Langdon's Purlieu, and she was certain that if she knew that truth, she would know the truth about Susan's death as well.

She sighed and went to her window to stare out. The fact was, the mystery of Susan's death was no longer her sole reason for wanting the truth. She wanted to know and understand Paul Langdon, and to help him if she could. And there was Varda, too — she loved Varda as though she were her own child and not her niece.

What was it that Paul had come so

close to telling her? Something so horrible that he could not bring himself to put it into words, not even after what he had already told her of his family. Did he believe Varda had inherited the family curse, the thirst for blood?

That was incredible, of course. Quite impossible if you looked at it rationally. But was he sufficiently irrational just now, with money problems and the death of his wife, that he thought this was the truth?

Or maybe it wasn't Varda at all. Maybe he thought the curse had tainted one of the others. His mother was out of the question. She was as harmless as the child, if a bit cold at times. Ray? She could no more imagine him harming anyone than she could imagine him flying to the moon. He was too much a playboy. The servants? But if that were the case, Paul had only to dismiss them. And anyway, he had talked of a family curse, and however close they might be, or however loyal, the servants simply were not family.

That, she thought, left only Paul himself — and that, too, was impossible. He was a hard man, yes, and difficult to get close to, but she couldn't really imagine him hurting someone intentionally.

She went back to the big chair and sat down, picturing Paul in her mind. Was it impossible that he was talking about himself when he talked of a blood curse? The thought kept returning unbidden to her mind. She had come here because Paul was suspect in Susan's death. She had known from the first time she saw him that he was a man of dark, brooding forces capable of acts that would seem brutal to others. In a fit of temper, to which he was certainly subject, he might conceivably do things that would later strike him as odious.

Her head ached from trying to make sense of it. Maria had warned her that very first day of danger here. Susan had written of danger as well, especially of danger from Paul. Paul himself had warned her of danger and told her of an old blood curse on the family.

She had certainly had ample warnings. Yet if that danger existed, it could surely only come from one source — Paul himself.

It was late and the room was cool. The fire had been laid but not lit, and there were matches on the mantel. When she picked them up she saw that they were commercial matches — according to the cover, from the Kristal Boarding House, where she had taken Cynthia Burke's place and waited for someone from the island to come for her.

She was sure these matches had not been there before. She closed her eyes and thought back. Yes, the matches on the mantle before had been in a little foil box, with no imprint on them. Had Maria left these by chance? Or had someone else left them, and did they have some special significance? Ray had been in town with her and she'd had the impression then that he was spying on her. Did he know who she was? And, if so, was this his subtle way of warning her?

She lit the fire, dropping the matchbook into her pocket. If they had been left here by mere chance, there was no point in calling them to anyone's attention. And if they had not, she would make it a point to be on her toes.

Doctor Morris had nearly convinced her that her concerns were foolish, but if Paul had managed nothing else, he had convinced her otherwise. Something was wrong here, in this house. There was danger here, of some as yet undefined sort. She was certain that in some way it had brought about Susan's death.

She did not intend that it should bring about hers as well.

* * *

Paul was withdrawn during dinner, his few contributions to the conversation formal and brief, but several times she glanced in his direction to find him watching her. Each time he looked quickly away, leaving her to wonder what really was on his mind. Was he regretting having told her so much? Or contemplating what else she ought to know?

Ray chatted almost incessantly and Jeannie tried to keep the conversation going with him, but she had the impression the people around the table were all under some kind of strain. Had

Paul told the others about his conversation with her? Perhaps they had discussed her at length. Perhaps all of them already knew who she was and even now were planning what they should do with her.

She knew that to lose one's nerve in any undertaking was to court disaster. People sensed fear, even hidden fear, and when they knew you were afraid they knew they had an advantage over you. She had learned that lesson early, from Max. She did not intend to give anyone that advantage ever again.

After dinner she joined Beatrice Langdon in the parlor and both worked on their embroidery, occasionally exchanging comments. Jeannie sensed, however, that Mrs. Langdon had more on her mind than idle comments, and she was soon enough proven right.

'Paul tells me he talked to you of our family skeletons,' she said after a time, without looking up from her handiwork.

Jeannie smiled tolerantly, hoping to convey that the legends had seemed rather trivial to her. 'All the Slavic vampires and ghouls, you mean?' she asked. 'It made for an interesting story, although a little too weird for my tastes.'

'Are you saying you don't take our history seriously?' Beatrice did look up at her then.

Jeannie looked up too and shook her head. 'No, not that part of it. I'm afraid I haven't much faith in things of that sort.'

Mrs. Langdon, however, looked neither amused nor reassured. 'Perhaps you ought not to dismiss them so lightly,' she said. 'There are many things that man does not yet understand, and much of what we do understand, men used to scoff at.'

Jeannie met her eyes without backing down. 'Do you think I ought to be afraid? Is that what you're trying to tell me, Mrs. Langdon?'

Beatrice surrendered first, looking back down at her embroidery. 'I'm only saying that people have believed in these things for centuries. Some very intelligent people, too, I might add. I'm not sure it behooves us to hold our modern viewpoints in such rigid esteem.'

'Mrs. Langdon, are you afraid of vampires?' Jeannie asked bluntly.

She was surprised when the older woman answered, without a moment's hesitation, 'Of course.'

Jeannie's smile vanished. 'And do you think there is danger of that sort here, on this island?'

'I wonder,' Beatrice said reflectively, 'if you ought to be here at all, Miss Burke. My son didn't want you brought here. Of course you know that. You remember how he went on when you arrived, and perhaps he was right. You're very young and very innocent, maybe even a little foolish. And certainly very beautiful. That's rather a dangerous combination of traits, I should think.'

'I don't know that I entirely agree with the inventory,' Jeannie said, a little stiffly. She did not like hearing that she was innocent or foolish, but especially she did not like the idea that Mrs. Langdon was thinking about dismissing her. *Whose safety is she thinking of*, she wondered, *mine or theirs?*

'Very beautiful indeed,' Beatrice went on as though talking to herself. 'A very great temptation for someone weak, someone longing for affection, for — '

'Well, here we are,' Ray said from the doorway. 'I hope I'm not crashing the party.'

Jeannie wanted to throw her sewing at his head, but Beatrice was completely herself again, even looking a bit non-plussed at what she had been saying.

'I was just telling Miss Burke,' she said, folding up her embroidery, 'that I think she is a very beautiful young woman.'

'Why, I've been telling her that since I first set eyes on her,' Ray said. 'Not that it's done me any good.'

'Well, they say one must keep trying.' Mrs. Langdon put her work back into her basket and stood, smoothing her skirt. There was nothing in her expression or manner to indicate that only a minute or so she had been talking about vampires and present dangers. 'I'm at least able to leave the field to you, if that helps, since it's time I retired. Good night, my dear,' she said to Jeannie. With a brief nod in her son's direction, she was gone, her footsteps vanishing down the corridor outside.

Jeannie was disappointed. She was certain Mrs. Langdon had been on the verge of telling her something more. Everyone here hinted, throwing her little crumbs of information, but always they stopped before they told her what she really wanted to know. Beatrice Langdon had surely been trying to give her another warning, and again the warning had been too vague to be of any real use.

'Say, you look like you could eat nails,' Ray said. 'I hope Mama hasn't been scaring you with her old stories. She's got a barrel of them, you know, from the old world. And when she runs dry, Franz always drags out a few new ones for her to chew on.'

Jeannie gave him a forced smile. His mother had said she was a great temptation, especially for someone weak, someone longing for affection. Certainly Ray was the weakest of the people on the island, and the most easily tempted. Was Beatrice trying to tell her that Ray was the one she should be afraid of?

'No,' she said aloud, 'she hasn't been scaring me, although I did hear a few old-world stories. About the Langdons, as a matter of fact.'

He scowled. 'So you heard all that rubbish about the vampires. The Langdon Beast. That's what they used in one of those tabloid stories years back. I was just a kid but I remember it well. Rather a gory bit of stuff, too. It takes its toll on you, growing up reading that sort of garbage about your own people.'

He spoke into the fireplace, his fists clenched at his side. It was the first she had ever thought of him as having a temper, and yet it was not surprising he should have one. He was Paul's brother, after all. She realized, too, as she looked at them, what strong hands he had. In many ways she thought Ray was probably a weakling, but not physically. Physically, she was sure he was very strong.

'That's exactly what it was, though — just garbage,' he said forcefully, slapping the mantel with the flat of one hand. When he turned to her again he was smiling his usual careless smile. 'You mustn't let it upset you,' he said.

'I won't,' she said, gathering her own

sewing. 'Only, I think your mother might be thinking of sending me away.'

He gave her a wink. 'Don't worry about that. I've about decided that I won't ever let you leave the island.'

When she thought about that remark later, in the safety of her bedroom, she decided she did not find it particularly reassuring.

13

She woke the following morning to a timid dawn. Maria arrived soon after with her coffee and petit-pains. The servant woman was always quiet and withdrawn, but today she wore an especially sullen look. Jeannie could not help thinking of her conversation the previous day with Paul, and how news of it had perturbed both Beatrice and Ray Langdon. She wondered if something might have been said to Maria as well.

'Maria,' she said before the woman could scurry away, 'you've been with the Langdon family a long time, haven't you?'

'Since my marriage, miss. Better than forty years it is now,' she said matter-of-factly.

'Then you must have been exposed to all the old stories.' She saw Maria stiffen but she hurried on. 'About vampires and the like. Weren't you ever frightened?'

When Maria turned back to look at

her, her eyes were wide with fright. She looked as though she expected some sort of ghoul to suddenly spring at her from the corner of the room.

'I promised myself I would speak only the once,' she said in a small voice, 'but you ought to go away from here, miss. There was a blood moon the night you came. It has marked you as a child of tragedy.'

'But what do I have to be afraid of?' Jeannie persisted.

'You must believe me — a dreadful fate stalks you through these halls. You are not safe here.' With that Maria hurried away before Jeannie could question her further.

Another warning, she thought morosely, sipping her coffee. She could almost believe it was a concerted effort to frighten her away. Well, it would take more than ominous and mysterious warnings to drive her from this island, she promised herself. She smiled. A dreadful fate indeed. Maria had been with the Langdons so long that all those old ghost stories had seeped into her brain. *And that is about as much value as they have,* she thought. Yesterday, depressed and influenced by Paul's silver burning eyes, it had been easy to attach importance to those old tales; but in the light of a fresh day she could only see how silly they were.

Vampires indeed! She wished Lou Benner, with his good, sound common sense, were here so she could tell him the whole business. What a laugh they would have together.

Somehow, though, the subject seemed less amusing when she came into the big kitchen later and found Varda waiting for her lessons. All the questions came back to her again. Something had happened here in this house, and she couldn't just dismiss that with a laugh. Susan had died, and there was something mysterious about her death.

Certainly Paul had spoken the truth when he said the Langdons weren't ordinary people. Varda wasn't being allowed to grow up in a normal fashion, and her father had hinted that there was something wrong with Varda — something dreadful, connected to the old legends. Surely that was only in his mind.

When she saw the child, she felt guilty for giving the slightest credence to such thoughts.

Varda was playing with the doll Jeannie had brought her from town, a pretty little creature with spun blonde hair that managed to talk, walk, drink, wet and probably, Jeannie thought with a suppressed grin, spin grisly yarns about the history of the Langdons.

She really did enjoy these morning lessons with Varda. The child was a blessing. Despite the odd life she lived, she had an apparently inexhaustible fountain of cheer that she gladly poured out for Jeannie's benefit. No matter how glum Jeannie felt when she came down, she always felt better in the girl's presence.

While they did their lessons, Maria worked away in her part of the big room, seemingly oblivious to their presence. Once or twice her husband, Franz, came in, bringing stores she had asked for, and once to remove a box that was in her way.

Jeannie found herself looking at the man with new curiosity. He was surly and uncommunicative, and of all the people on the island, the one she would most be inclined to fear. Was it possible she was being warned against him? But surely the Langdons were masters of their own home. And it was obvious that Franz was slavishly devoted to the family.

Once, Franz turned to find her eyes on him. A chill went through her as if someone had walked over her grave. His eyes were heartless and cruel. Yet she had seen them soften with feeling, even genuine devotion — but not for his wife; that had been for the Langdons, especially for Beatrice Langdon.

So he was not a man totally beyond conventional feelings, even if his life had left him hard and bitter. Perhaps he had shared the shame of the Langdons. Perhaps as their chief contact with the outside world, he had suffered more embarrassment and mockery than they themselves had.

Of one thing she was certain — he had no love for anyone or anything but the Langdons and their island. These were his life. As for his wife, if she meant anything to him at all, it was as a gift for the Langdons, an acquisition that permitted him to serve them with four hands instead of two.

Jeannie had gotten into the habit of taking Varda outside to the courtyard for a brief time each morning, so the child got some fresh air and sunshine. At least in the courtyard Jeannie didn't feel they had to watch their conversation so closely, either. No one was likely to hear them from the house and it would have been difficult for anyone to join them unnoticed.

Up to this time Jeannie had not tried to discuss Varda's mother with her, not wanting to disturb the child with unpleasant memories that must still be fresh in her young mind. The previous day's conversations, however, had left her with too many questions, and if she was ever to help Varda — really help her — those questions must somehow be answered.

'Varda,' she said as nonchalantly as she could, 'you never talk about your mother. I hope you haven't forgotten her.'

Varda gave her a guarded look and Jeannie wondered if she might have been warned against this subject, but she said, 'I remember her. She was very pretty.'

'And was she very nice?'

'Yes,' Varda said, somewhat hesitantly. 'Only, she was very nervous.'

The doctor had told Jeannie about Susan's mental state and her reliance upon drugs; and Ray, too, had commented on Susan's nerves. She had no doubt Susan had been a disappointing mother.

'It must be sad for you to have her gone.'

Varda nodded vaguely, concentrating on her coloring book. When she made no reply, Jeannie went on cautiously. 'Do you remember when she left you?'

Varda gave her head an emphatic shake. 'I was asleep.'

'But surely you must remember something,' Jeannie insisted.

Varda looked up at her with a puzzled expression, as though she had gone over this same thing many times before. 'I don't remember,' she said in a voice that pleaded for belief. 'I was asleep and people came and looked at me. My grandmother was there, and my father and Maria, and grandmother was crying and kissing me, but I couldn't wake up at first. And when I did, they told me my mama was gone.' She began to cry.

'Oh, poor darling,' Jeannie said, grabbing her in a fervent embrace. 'I'm sorry, pet, I didn't mean to make you cry. Forgive me, please. We won't talk about it any more.'

To her relief, Varda's tears stopped on the instant, and her natural high spirits returned. She hugged Jeannie back and said, 'Mama always said I was just a baby.'

'I don't think you're a baby at all. I think you're a very fine young woman.'

'I'm glad you came,' Varda said, snuggling against her shoulder. 'I prayed for you to come, so I wouldn't have to be so lonely.'

It was Jeannie's turn to fight back tears.

★   ★   ★

The first thing she saw when she went into her room soon after was the shattered mirror. Ray had hung it for her and she had waited defiantly for some comment to be made. None had been, and now it was shattered into a thousand pieces, the broken slivers of glass scattered on the floor. Too angry to be frightened, she pulled the cord that summoned Maria.

'What do you know about this?' she demanded when Maria came into her room a few minutes later.

Maria looked at the glass and back at Jeannie. 'I do not understand,' she said. 'It looks like you have broken your looking-glass.'

'I didn't break it,' Jeannie nearly shouted.

Maria only looked all the more puzzled. 'But I can see for myself, it is all over . . . '

'Someone else broke it,' Jeannie snapped. 'Someone came into my room while I was downstairs and deliberately — ' She caught herself in mid-sentence. She had no right to yell at the servant. Either Maria knew nothing about this, or if she did, she had no intention of admitting the fact. 'Oh, never mind,' she said. 'I'm sorry. This will have to be cleaned up. Where will I find a broom and dustpan?'

'I will get them,' Maria said, obviously relieved to have the brief inquisition ended. She left and was back in a few minutes with the needed equipment. Together they set about cleaning up the broken glass.

While they worked, Ray appeared at the open door. 'I thought I heard yelling,' he said, stepping into the room. He saw the broken glass then and the empty frame on the wall where he had hung the mirror. 'Hey, what happened to that?'

'Someone broke it,' Jeannie said from the floor. 'And I . . . ouch.' She jumped as a splinter of glass stuck in her finger. She plucked it out and threw it into the wastebasket.

Ray quickly knelt beside her, taking her hand in his. A drop of blood had appeared where the glass splinter had been. He stared at it as though fascinated. 'You know,' he said, looking up to grin at Jeannie, 'according to all the legends, I should be quite charmed by that sight. And I should feel an irresistible urge to kiss your wounded finger.' He looked at it again and his grin widened. 'As a matter of fact, I do feel an irresistible urge to kiss your finger.' He did just that.

Another time she would have regarded this as only another display of his harmless inanity, but today she pulled her hand away from his uneasily. 'You know,' she said, casting a glance at Maria, who was ignoring them, 'I'm only an employee here. It wouldn't do for you to forget who I am.'

'I assure you, dear lady,' he said, 'now that I know who you are, I shall never forget it.'

Just what he meant by that remark she could not judge from his laughing expression. Maria had finished with the clean-up and started for the door. Ray stood as if to go also, but he paused for a moment. 'You ought to put something on that finger,' he said. 'You never know what you might pick up here.' He winked at her and left.

She stared after him, his remark ringing in her ears. Had it been only an innocent comment, or did he truly know who she was? And if he did, what did he intend to do about it? If he kept it to himself, there would be no great harm done, surely. But if he told his brother . . . she had no doubt Paul would be furious. He would order her to leave at once, she had no doubt of that. She would never find out what she had come here to learn.

And, she thought sadly, she would lose Paul forever.

She went to the dresser for a tissue to press against the tiny cut. It was hardly serious enough to require any dressing.

There, atop the dresser, was another book of matches from the boarding house in the village, the boarding house at which she and Cynthia Burke had exchanged places and names. She clutched the matchbook tightly in her fingers and looked at the mirror frame hanging forlornly empty on one wall.

For the first time she felt truly afraid. Maria was right with her muttered warnings, no matter how embellished they were by old-world myth.

She was in danger here.

14

Looking back, it seemed to Jeannie that
Ray had not been particularly surprised
to find the mirror broken. Of course he
must have expected something like that
all along. After all, he was the one who
had suggested that she not mention it to
the others. That would indicate that he
had not broken it, wouldn't it? Why go to
the bother of hanging it for her if he
intended to smash it later? And if he had
not done so, who had? Beatrice was the
obvious suspect. Ray had told her that his
mother had a fetish regarding mirrors.

That explanation seemed a little too
pat, however. Still, what other explanation
was there? Someone — and no phantom,
either, but someone quite physical and
real — had smashed her mirror. And one
motive made about as much sense as
another.

One thing she did promise herself: she
would not bring up the subject of the

broken mirror. If it was smashed to frighten her away, someone would be disappointed. A few pieces of shattered glass were not going to send her running.

As for the matches, this time she did not even remove them but left them where they were. It might be that whoever left them did not know anything but only suspected. Let them think the match cover had no significance for her and perhaps they would suspect less.

Throughout the rest of the day she managed to act as though nothing unusual had occurred. Nor did any of the family give any indication to the contrary. When she retired that night to her room, however, she was uneasy.

She tried to read but found her attention wandering. At last, restless, she took a lamp with her and left her room. The parlor was empty and dark. A light in the kitchen told her Maria was still at work there, and another light behind the closed door of Paul's study told her where he was. There was no sign of the others. Presumably Beatrice had gone up to bed.

She took her coat from the hall and

draping it about her shoulders, let herself out into the courtyard, thinking some fresh air would help to calm her restlessness. It was a dark night, with only a few brave stars peeking through the clouds above. She went to the fountain and sat on its rim, putting the lamp on the tiles beside her.

The water in the fountain had frozen and thawed several times since she'd been here. It was thawed now, although still winter-cold. She ran her fingers through it idly and looked up at the dim faces of the naiads. They looked back at her in amusement. She wondered at the secret that brought those cunning smiles to their faces. Old Neptune was as grim as ever. His solemn visage seemed to echo the warnings she had already been given, warnings to leave Langdon's Purlieu.

'Perhaps I should heed the warnings,' she whispered to him. She met his cold gaze for a moment, and shook her head. 'No, that would be admitting defeat. I'll stay, and in the end I'll get what I want.'

The naiads greeted her pronouncement with unrestrained mirth.

Behind her the shutters were suddenly opened upon the lighted windows of Paul's study, sending the light splashing across the stones of the courtyard. She turned guiltily toward the windows, but he had not seen her. He was talking over his shoulder to his brother and he turned his back on her without seeing her by the fountain.

She made a move to go, but Paul's words arrested her. ' . . . I won't let her leave the island,' he said emphatically.

She sat back down, cringing back into the shadows. They were speaking about her, she was sure of it.

Ray's reply was lost to her, and Paul's next remark was muffled as he had moved away from the window. She struggled with her conscience. Should she go back inside, or move nearer to the window where she could hear their conversation better?

In the end, her need to discover the truth won. She rose and moved stealthily closer to the window, careful to avoid the rectangle of bright light that fell from within.

Ray was speaking. ' . . . the same thing that happened to your wife.'

'Who are you to say that wasn't an accident?' Paul asked.

Jeannie flattened herself against a wall, her heart pounding so violently she was sure they must hear it inside the room.

'It was no accident,' Ray said with a small, dry laugh. 'We both know that.'

'All right then,' Paul said after a pause. 'Let's leave it at that. It was no accident.'

The stone was damp and cold beneath her hands. In the distance she heard the pounding of the waves upon rocky cliffs, and nearer, the gentle murmur of the fountain. A scent of fresh bread drifted out from the kitchen where Maria still worked.

Susan's death was not an accident. She felt torn in two. Part of her had always insisted this and that part was glad to be confirmed, but another part of her wanted to burst into tears.

She shook her head, trying to drive away the thoughts clamoring within, and brought her attention back to the conversation inside.

'If she stays, it will be just like Susan,' Ray said.

'I won't let her go,' Paul said again. He came to the window. Jeannie pressed still tighter against the wall.

'Damn,' Paul said from within. Suddenly she remembered the lamp she had left behind by the fountain. It gleamed its alarm without wavering, where he could hardly fail to see it when he looked. And that he had seen it she knew when he called out, 'Who's there?'

She held her breath and a moment later she heard his footsteps quickly crossing the room toward the hall.

She turned and ran. The nearest escape from the courtyard was the gate that led to the landing. She fled down the thick stone steps, her coat flying behind her. The cold wind, unhindered here by stone walls, tore at her hair and threatened to freeze the tears on her lashes.

Something moved suddenly, a shadow darker than the others. She cried out without thinking and tried to turn aside, but she was caught in the grip of strong hands and she found herself staring up into the cruel face of Franz.

'What are you doing down here?' he demanded.

'Let me go,' she cried, struggling against him. She didn't know whether he had angered or frightened her more, but she knew she did not like being held in his grip so tightly that her arms ached.

'Who's there?' Paul called from above. 'Franz, is that you?'

'*Ja*,' he called back, releasing his hold on Jeannie. A moment later Paul came down the steps, his face an angry mask. His eyes flashed when he saw her.

'What are you doing here?' he demanded, echoing Franz.

She gave her head a toss. 'I couldn't sleep,' she said, 'so I came out for some air and I came down here to look at the water, thinking it would be restful.'

'You know I don't like you prowling around at night,' he said.

She swept by him as grandly as she could manage, her chin painfully high. 'And I don't like being attacked and mauled in the dark, nor spoken to like a naughty child,' she replied over her shoulder.

He did not intend to be put off that easily. He came after her, taking two steps to her one. 'Is that your lamp by the fountain?' he asked.

'Of course it's my lamp. Who do you think put it there, one of your family ghosts?'

They reached the top of the steps and went into the courtyard side by side.

'Then you were listening at my windows.'

'I think you're very rude,' she said, picking up her lamp. 'What makes you think I would want to sneak around listening at windows? And anyway,' she added, turning to look in the direction of his windows, 'those shutters were closed, as I remember, when I came out.' *And so far*, she thought, *I haven't exactly had to tell a lie.*

She did not mean to give him the opportunity to force her into one. She went past him again, toward the hall door, ignoring Ray who had come to the windows and was watching their little scene with obvious amusement.

'I must ask you again not to go

wandering about at night,' Paul called after her, sounding angrier than ever. 'Don't force me to take drastic steps.'

She stopped and turned on him, giving vent to some of her own anger. 'Such as what?' she demanded. 'Do you intend to put a bolt outside my door and lock me in at night the way you do your daughter? Be careful, Mr. Langdon — I am not your prisoner and I won't be made one.'

Paul turned white but he said nothing in reply. Ray applauded loudly. 'Bravo,' he called. 'I think you've met your match, brother mine. I told you she had a fiery temper, that one.'

She turned on him, his mocking humor only making her angrier still. 'And you,' she cried, 'just . . . ' But she couldn't think of anything appropriate to his delighted laughter. She whirled about instead and ran inside, thinking of nothing more than escaping Ray's laughter and Paul's burning eyes.

15

She had scarcely reached her room, slamming the door after herself and throwing herself across her bed, when there was a knock at her door. She opened it to find Ray outside.

'The show is over,' she said, moving to close the door.

He held it open. He was smiling now, but in his usual friendly fashion. 'Sorry if I got your goat,' he said. 'It's just that I'm not used to seeing my brother bested. He's in love with you, you know.'

She blushed and looked away from his mocking eyes. 'I think you're imagining things,' she said. 'The only emotion your brother feels toward me is rather frequent anger.'

'Don't fool yourself. But a friendly bit of advice — having Paul in love with you can be a dangerous state of affairs.'

She looked up, angry all over again. 'Another warning? Everybody about this place keeps busy giving me vague and mysterious warnings, but no one ever wants to explain.'

His sober mood passed again. 'I haven't told him, in case you're worried.'

'Told him what?'

'Our little secret,' he said with a wink.

She gave a quick start. 'I'm not aware that we have any secrets, little or big,' she said, but she knew he had noticed her surprise.

He suddenly took hold of her shoulders and pulled her close to him. 'There's more to Susan's death than you've been told,' he said in a low voice. 'Be careful, little lady.' Then, before she could reply, he kissed her.

When the kiss was ended, the first thing she saw was Paul standing a few feet away down the hall, looking at them. His eyes met hers for only an instant. Then, with a mumbled, 'Excuse me,' he had gone by them and around the corner.

'Sorry,' Ray said, letting her go, 'but I had to do that so my brother wouldn't be suspicious of our little conversation. Anyway, I rather enjoyed it.' He gave her a wave of his hand and went quickly down the hall in the opposite direction from his brother, leaving her completely dumbfounded at her door.

She dreamed of Paul that night. He stood waiting for her on a windy cliff, but when she came up to him, he turned his back on her.

By morning her sense of uneasiness had grown. She had a vague impression that events were moving them along inexorably, toward some climax that she could not foresee. If she had been more superstitious, she might have said the omens were inauspicious.

She did not know, however, what she could or should do to halt the tide of events. The conversation she had overheard the night before had answered some questions and raised others. Yes, she knew now that Susan's death was not an accident, as she had suspected all along — both brothers had agreed on that. But she did not yet know what really had happened, and she felt so close to this answer that she could hardly want to run away now, before she learned the full truth.

On the other hand, she had to face the fact that she was now genuinely frightened here. She was aware of her own limitations. If violence threatened, what could she do? She had no clear ally to whom she could turn. She did not even know who exactly her enemy was. Even if some member of the family proved to be entirely innocent — Beatrice Langdon, for instance — she was not likely to turn against her sons and side with an outsider against them. And the servants were completely loyal to the family.

Maybe she really should leave — but if she did, the mystery she had come here to solve would remain forever unravelled. No, she could not leave until she had discovered the truth.

The day that had begun with an unsettled atmosphere did not improve as it went along. It got worse with the incident of Varda's doll.

Since Jeannie had brought the doll from town, Varda had kept it with her almost constantly. The doll had never missed a school lesson. So, noticing the doll's absence this particular morning,

Jeannie had to ask about it.

'Where's Baby?' she asked, indicating the seat where the doll usually sat beside Varda.

Varda did not even look up when she said, 'Baby's dead.'

'Varda,' Jeannie said, shocked, 'what a thing to say. Where is she?'

'She fell on the rocks,' Varda said, beginning to cry, 'and died.'

Maria took something from the wood box near where she worked and brought it silently over to Jeannie. It was the doll, but it had indeed been hopelessly smashed. Half of her face was gone, and one arm. There were no fingers on the remaining hand, and the legs were held on by a few straggling wires.

Varda was crying into her hands, not even looking at the doll. Jeannie motioned for Maria to come with her into the hall. 'What happened to this?' she asked when they were out of Varda's hearing.

Maria looked genuinely unhappy and for once she spoke without any apparent resentment. 'The young miss went up to the turret to play. She is not supposed to go there but sometimes she just forgets. It looks like she accidentally dropped the doll from the window and it broke into a hundred pieces when it landed in the court-yard.'

'Oh, dear.' Jeannie examined the battered doll, but there was no hope of repairing it. She would have to look for another one in town, only not immedi-ately. Varda would only resent an immediate replacement.

'It is almost like when her mother died,' Maria said with a cluck of her tongue.

Yes, Jeannie thought, it did sound the same. Even Varda had not said that the doll fell to the courtyard and broke, but that it had fallen on the rocks and died. She thought of the lonely girl's unhappy life here, locked in her room, frightened by stories of family curses — so few chances for any happiness. Had Varda re-enacted the scene of her mother's death out of some morbid obsession?

It was this unpleasant thought that drove her to seek out Paul after lunch. She was painfully aware of his coolness toward her but she ignored that. She was thinking of Varda's well-being now and she must not let her personal emotions interfere.

'I've come to talk to you about Varda,' she said, standing before the desk in his den.

'It's my impression that you're doing a very good job with her,' he said in a business-like voice. 'She not only appears to be learning well but she seems happier, too. And although some of my actions must seem peculiar to her, I do care about my daughter's happiness.'

'I'm certain of that or I wouldn't be standing here now. But I don't think Varda is happy at all, if you'll pardon my saying so. Perhaps with my coming here to look after her she's a little less unhappy, but I don't think that's enough. I don't think the life she is living now is a particularly appropriate one for a child.'

He studied her with no expression. 'And what do you suggest should be done?' he asked.

'I think she should be taken off this island,' she said firmly. 'There are a

213

number of fine schools she could attend not far away and some of them are relatively inexpensive. It would cost you less to keep her in a good school than to hire tutors for her here, in fact. And after all, I can only teach her so much. She'll soon be at the point where she will need more advanced training than I can give her.'

'When that time comes,' he said, folding his hands together with an air of finality, 'we shall simply have to hire more advanced tutors. I'm afraid the idea of Varda going away to school is quite out of the question. But again, I thank you for the excellent job you've done.'

'But why is it out of the question?' she asked stubbornly. 'You do care about her, I know that, and surely you too can see the harm that's being done.'

'My daughter must remain on Langdon's Purlieu,' he said again. He went to the door and opened it. 'And now, if you'll excuse me, I have some rather important correspondence that I must attend to.'

★ ★ ★

As it happened, that same correspondence produced the argument that came up that evening at dinner.

'I've been corresponding with a New York investment firm,' Paul announced midway through the meal. 'They've made rather a handsome offer for the island. It seems a group of buyers would be interested in making it into a resort.'

Beatrice smiled tolerantly. 'Can you imagine, hordes of strangers tramping about on our island?' she said to Ray. 'Fat old men with golf clubs and fatter old women with whining dogs.'

'I'm afraid it may come to that,' Paul said, not at all amused. 'I've asked for a slightly higher price. If they meet my terms, I may sell.'

She turned pale. 'You can't do that,' she said angrily. 'I won't let you.'

He remained unmoved by her anger. 'You can't prevent it, as you well know.'

She stared at him for a moment in cold silence. When she spoke again it was in a less combative tone. 'But, why?' she asked. 'Why would you even consider it?'

'It's quite simple, really. We can no longer afford to keep up this place. The truth is, we haven't been able to afford it for a number of years. The Nova Scotia house is much smaller and easier to maintain. If we sell everything but that, we can live in comfort the rest of our lives instead of scraping by from month to month the way we have been.'

'Things have been better lately than they were for years,' Ray said.

To Jeannie's surprise, he too seemed dismayed at the prospect of losing the island. None of them were even aware of her presence just now. She studied Paul's face and realized that despite the mask he wore, this decision would be more painful for him than for either of the others.

'That's only because of Susan's money,' he said bluntly. 'But it just isn't enough to take care of everything.'

'She left a trust for Varda,' Beatrice said, plainly agitated. 'Can't we use that somehow?'

Paul shook his head. 'Don't be foolish. We can't touch that.'

She banged her hand down hard on the table, making the china and crystal rattle. 'That woman!' she exclaimed. 'How I hated her. Even in death she's managed to keep her precious money away from us.'

'Mother!' Paul said. For the first time since the argument had begun he looked at Jeannie. 'You must forgive us this family quarrel. It is ended now.' He gave his mother and brother stern looks.

His mother was not so easily silenced, though. 'You're forgetting just one thing. The Nova Scotia house isn't isolated from people the way this one is. That might be a problem, might it not?'

Jeannie could see that the remark hit home with Paul, although she did not know just why. For a fleeting moment he looked indecisive. Then, with a mocking grin, he said, 'Our tutor seems to feel that Varda ought to leave the island anyway. Perhaps she may be right.'

Beatrice returned his grin with one of her own, cold and vicious. 'You don't dare,' she said in a warning voice.

Ray stepped into the breach, leaning

across the table toward Jeannie. 'Nova Scotia is only a little colder than here,' he said flippantly. 'I don't think you'll find it too awfully extreme.'

'Am I to be crated up and shipped along with the furniture?' she asked.

'But of course. Our most precious possession.' He laughed and looked at his brother, whose face was dark.

16

Jeannie was surprised when Franz returned from his trip to town the next day with a letter for her — a letter actually addressed to Cynthia Burke. She looked at the envelope, wondering for a moment if this might be something personal for the real Cynthia Burke, but then she recognized the handwriting and, leaving Varda in Maria's care, she took the letter to her room to read.

It was from Lou Benner and it was brief. 'I'm at the hotel in the village. Can you make it in to see me?' There was no signature and no name as a greeting. Nothing in the note could incriminate her. Nonetheless, she tore it into tiny pieces and scattered them out the window before she went in search of the family.

She found Ray and his mother in the courtyard, engaged in earnest discussion. Probably, she guessed, having to do with Paul's plans to sell the island. They stopped talking at once when they saw her approaching and she could not help thinking that they had instinctively placed her on Paul's side. In a way it was flattering, but she wished that Paul himself felt that way about her.

'I'm afraid an unexpected errand has come up,' she said. 'I wonder if it would be possible for me to go into town this afternoon?'

'I'm sure it could be arranged,' Beatrice said. She raised one eyebrow. 'Nothing serious, I hope.'

Jeannie gave her an innocent smile. 'No, only a little personal business,' she said.

Beatrice accepted the closed door graciously. 'We'll have Franz take you across. I suppose you would like to go soon?'

'I'll just get my coat,' Jeannie said. 'And thank you.'

When she came down a short time later the Langdons were not about but Franz was waiting for her at the landing. He looked less gracious about this second trip of the day than Beatrice had been, but Jeannie did not concern herself greatly with his surly mood. She was more interested in seeing Lou again and learning what had brought him here.

She found him in the hotel lobby. His familiar and concerned face was a welcome sight. She had nearly forgotten the pleasure of knowing you could count on someone's friendship and loyalty without doubt or question.

'Lou,' she said, embracing him happily. 'What a welcome sight you are.'

'And you too. I was afraid they had chained you in a dungeon,' he said. 'I wanted to come sooner but I was tied up in court. I've been worried since Miss Burke showed up with your check.'

'You did take care of her all right? I'd feel awful if the poor girl didn't get what I'd promised her.'

Lou led her off to a corner of the lobby where they were unlikely to be overheard. 'Yes, Miss Burke is fine. As a matter of fact I made it a point to check on her before I came. Her mother's operation was a success and she's recovering nicely, thanks to you.'

'I'm glad,' Jeannie said sincerely, sitting beside him on a small leather-covered sofa.

He gave her a quick scrutiny. 'And what about your operation?' he asked.

'Not completely successful,' she admitted ruefully, 'but not a complete flop either.' She told him briefly what she had learned since her arrival at the island, limiting herself as much as possible to the facts concerning Susan's death. There was no reason, she told herself, to burden Lou with her emotional problems.

Lou's expression grew increasingly troubled as he listened to her story. He frowned but did not interrupt until she had brought him up to date.

'So,' she concluded, 'it seems like I'm on the verge of learning the whole story, if I can just stay on my toes for a short time longer.'

'I don't like any of this, you know,' he said. 'I'd have gotten in touch with you as soon as I learned you were here, only I didn't want to make anyone suspicious.'

'I know,' she said, giving his knee a reassuring pat. 'But as long as I keep my wits about me, I can't be in too much danger.'

'I'm not so sure. I may as well tell you what I've learned since I arrived. I doubt that your identity is any secret to the Langdons. At least to one of them. The son, Ray, knows you're Susan's sister. I checked around town myself and found out he made inquiries about you.'

She nodded. 'I expected as much, but I don't think he's told the others. And I don't believe I have to worry about Ray. I'm certain he's harmless.'

'Jeannie, I wish you wouldn't go back to that place,' Lou said. 'Or at least not alone. If you have to return, then at least let me go along. We'll confront them with our suspicions and demand the truth.'

'And be ordered off the island,' she said, shaking her head. 'No, Lou, this is the only way we'll ever know the whole story, believe me.'

He sighed deeply. 'Very well, then. But I am going to make certain conditions. I'm going to stay on here for a few days, just in case you need me close at hand. Tell me, could you drive one of those boats if you had to?'

'I think so.'

'Well, if anything bad happens, anything that seems really threatening, I want you to leave at once. Will you promise me that?'

She hesitated, knowing that Lou would take decisive action on his own if he thought it necessary to protect her. 'All right,' she agreed. 'I promise.'

'And,' he said, taking a quick look around to be sure they were unwatched, 'I want you to keep this with you.' He brought a small revolver from his pocket and dropped it quickly into her bag. 'Chances are you'll never have to use it, but it's a good thing to have on hand, just in case. If nothing else, it may give somebody a good scare.'

'Me especially,' she said. 'I'd probably shoot my own toe off.' But she was grateful for the reassuring weight when she picked the bag up. 'I'd better go,' she said, giving him her hand. 'I'll try to send a letter or get in touch within the next few days.'

She looked back from the front door.

Lou was still standing in the same spot, looking anxiously after her. She waved to him and went out — and found Franz waiting on the sidewalk just outside.

'What are you doing here?' she asked. She had left him at the landing.

'It is getting late,' he said gruffly, starting off down the street. 'We must start back.'

She walked quickly after him, annoyed and frightened to think he had been spying on her. Had he seen Lou put the gun in her purse? She couldn't remember what sort of interior view the front window afforded and she couldn't go back now to look. 'How did you know where I was?' she asked.

'Small town,' he said, leaving her to interpret that as she wished.

It was nearly night when they arrived back at the island. Jeannie went straight to her room to clean up and change for dinner, but she had scarcely gotten into a fresh dress when Maria appeared, looking concerned.

'The little miss is asking for you,' she said. 'She wants to see you.'

'She's all right, isn't she?'

'Yes, but . . . ' Maria paused, discretion fighting with her affection for the child. 'She had a dream, she says. She says she has to tell you something.'

Jeannie breathed a sigh of relief. 'Well, it will only take a minute, but you had better play chaperone, in case her father hears of it.'

Varda was still in her nightgown, having just awakened from a late nap, but she had a serious look on her face.

'Hello, darling,' Jeannie greeted her with a hug. 'What's this Maria tells me about a bad dream?'

Varda shook her head. 'Not a bad dream,' she said solemnly, 'but it was a dream about you. A voice came to me while I was asleep and said that my Mommy wanted you.'

Jeannie cast a quick glance at Maria but she only looked confused and uncertain. 'Your mommy?' Jeannie said.

'Yes, the voice said she wanted you to come to the attic in the west wing. There is a message there.'

'Well, it sounds like a very important

message,' Jeannie said.

'It is,' Varda assured her. 'The voice in my dream said so. And it said you were to come at once.'

Although she tried to keep her face composed, Jeannie's thoughts were racing. Was this really only a dream? Or as it some sort of mysterious plot to . . . to what? She shook her head. She was becoming as silly as the Langdons with all their superstitions.

'Tell me, darling,' she asked, 'was this voice a woman's voice or a man's?' Behind her Maria gasped, but Jeannie kept her eyes on Varda's

Varda only shrugged uncomprehendingly. 'It was an angel's voice,' she said, as though that ought to be clear to anyone. 'Only angels can talk to you in dreams.'

Jeannie gave her another hug and a kiss. 'Well, thank you, darling, for delivering your message so punctually. Now you just put it out of your mind, promise?'

'I promise,' Varda said, relieved to have done her duty.

At the door, Maria gave Jeannie a worried look. 'We do not go into the west wing,' she said in a whisper.

Jeannie already knew that. Ray had explained that the rooms there were primarily unfurnished and unrestored. Back in her own room, she sat for a moment puzzling over the strange message.

Surely Varda could not just have imagined it, although she was an imaginative child. But if she hadn't imagined it, where had the message come from? Sleep-talk? At some point in one of her therapies, Susan had gone through that process. She was placed under hypnosis and while she slept deeply, instructions were whispered into her ear; instructions that went, so the theory was, directly to the subconscious. Someone might have spoken to Varda while she slept, giving her this mysterious message and knowing she would deliver it when awake. But who, and why?

Finally she took a lamp and stole from her room. The halls were dark. The family would be gathering downstairs for dinner, but she knew her curiosity would not let her alone until she had investigated

— and what better time to do it than now, when everyone else would be in the parlor?

She had never been to the west wing of the house, but it was not difficult to find her way. She found herself in a succession of empty rooms that had quite obviously been unused for many years. At one point she knelt down to run her finger over the floor. The dust was thick and had not been disturbed for some time. Certainly nobody was waiting here for her. It would be impossible to cross through these rooms without leaving tracks as conspicuous as the ones she was leaving.

She had been wondering how she was even supposed to find an attic, when she came upon what must have been at one time a second library. At one end of the room rickety steps led upward to a closed wooden door. She paused at the bottom of the steps. They looked so plainly unsafe, she thought it would be folly to trust them.

Suddenly a beam of light spilled from the crack beneath the door. It flickered, moved away, and then returned. Someone was up there, moving about with a light. For a crazy moment she wondered if it could be Susan, but she rejected that idea at once. Spirits didn't come back to prowl the earth. Whoever was in that room above her, it was someone flesh and blood, just as real as she was. Someone who meant to frighten her.

Moreover, they were just as heavy as she was too. There was no one in this house, with the exception of Varda, who weighed less than she did. If these steps could support her would-be ghost, they could support her as well. She set the lamp on the floor, where it would light her way up the stairs, and went angrily upward.

She did not reach the door with its flickering light, however. The steps proved as flimsy as her first estimate of them. They jerked sickeningly and suddenly, even as she grabbed out for support, tore loose from the wall and sent her crashing downward.

17

She dreamed of the Langdon Beast. It held her in its powerful arms, carrying her along dimly lit halls. Once she opened her eyes and looked up, to discover that the face above her was Paul's and he was carrying her along the halls of the house.

Afterward, though, he melted into the rest of the dream. He was the Beast again and she felt those sharp teeth upon her. Her flesh was open, her vital forces draining from her. She struggled to escape the nightmare but strong hands held her back.

'Hush, don't move. Lie still.'

She did lie still. The dream had gone. After a moment or two she opened her eyes. Again it was Paul over her, looking down with great concern in his eyes. 'It's all right,' he said softly, holding her back when she tried to struggle to a sitting position. 'Just rest. I'm here.'

And knowing that he was there, she did

rest. She drifted back to sleep, a sleep this time free of nightmares.

When she awakened again he was still there, dozing in the wing chair that he had pulled over from the fire. He woke too when she stirred and sat up, blinking his eyes. 'Feel better?' he asked.

She smiled wanly and nodded. Her left arm ached and when she looked she discovered it was in bandages. As she became more fully awake she began to identify other spots that were most certainly bruised, if not worse.

'It seems we just get you out of one bandage in time to apply a fresh one,' he said, nodding at her arm. 'You were very lucky, though. No really serious damage.' He put on his serious look. 'If you're going to insist on flaunting every rule I lay down, you're going to have a lot of jolts. I warned you about rambling around by yourself. There are many unsafe places in this house.'

'I didn't just go rambling,' she said frankly. 'I was sent there.'

He looked surprised. 'Sent there? By whom?'

'By someone who was waiting in that

attic overhead, who knew I'd start up the stairs and have an accident.'

She told him about the message from Varda that had sent her into the unsafe wing of the house, and the light in the attic that had beckoned her.

'And you thought I was responsible?' he asked, staring hard at her.

She met his gaze without flinching. 'No,' she said honestly. 'For a long time I wondered about . . . about many things, but I don't believe you would deliberately set out to hurt me.'

What he thought about that remark she couldn't tell. 'But you thought I hurt my wife? You think I murdered her, don't you?'

The silence stretched wide between them, but at last, having searched deep within herself, she was able to say, 'No. I don't know what did happen, but I don't believe you murdered her.'

This time his relief was evident in his eyes. 'I didn't,' he said. 'I didn't love her, but I didn't murder her. I prayed you would come to realize that.'

She did not ask why it mattered to him what she believed. The answer to that was evident in his eyes as well. And he was a man who would expect you to know his feelings and believe in them without the necessity for a thousand words of reminder. Whatever he felt for you would remain real and solid.

'If you didn't love her, why did you marry her?'

He clasped his hands in his lap and looked down at them as though thinking this out for the first time himself. 'It wasn't entirely for the money, regardless of what you might have thought,' he said. 'I had lived in the shadows for so long. The shadows of this house. The shadows of my father's sickness. The shadows of my financial burden. And then I met Susan while I was in New York on business. She seemed to take to me at once, and she was so bright, so beautiful, so sparkling — it was like having the curtains suddenly ripped open on a dark room, so that the sunlight bursts in like an explosion. I knew from the first that I didn't love her, but she was the brightest, loveliest thing that had happened to me for so long.'

He paused and looked at her, his eyes pleading silently for understanding. 'Yes, I knew about the money. Maybe subconsciously that influenced me more than I realized, but when I brought her here, I truly thought she would brighten up this place. But she didn't have your indomitable spirits. The gloom of this island was stronger than her good cheer. It was bad almost from the start. She realized I didn't love her even before I did. And she didn't love me either. I was a substitute for a father she had just lost.'

Jeannie listened in sympathetic silence. She could understand everything that he had told her. No one could have been brighter and more dazzling than Susan when she chose to be. She could see the two of them drawn inexorably together by their mutual needs of the moment. And she could see, too, how quickly that would disintegrate. It would have taken only a few weeks in this place for Susan, weak and childish as she was, to have changed her mind and her heart completely.

Paul Langdon was not a man to admit defeat, however. She knew without asking that he did not believe in divorce. He was a man who, once he had given his word, held to it through thick or thin. He had given his word in a marriage contract, and only death would ever end that marriage for him.

'I should have let her go when she wanted to leave,' he said, spreading his hands in a gesture of frustration. 'She might be alive now.' He paused again and she thought he was on the verge of telling her about Susan's death, but he only finished by repeating, 'I didn't kill her.'

He stood and went to the bell that summoned Maria. When she appeared a minute later he said something to her Jeannie could not hear. Then he came back to the bed and clasped her hand briefly. 'I'm going to have a look at that attic,' he said. 'Maria will stay here with you. You can trust her.'

When he was gone, Maria took his place in the wing chair. She sat with her hands in her lap, eyes half-closed. There was nothing in her face to reveal how she felt about watching over Jeannie, but Jeannie told herself that Paul had said she could trust Maria. And by implication, he had admitted that she could not necessarily trust anyone else.

While he was gone, both Beatrice and Ray came in at different times. Beatrice was polite, but there was an air of disapproval in her manner. She seemed miffed that Jeannie should have had her accident, and she stayed only long enough to say she was glad Jeannie wasn't seriously hurt and that in the future she ought to heed Paul's advice and not go wandering about by herself.

Ray was more cheerful, of course, but curious. 'What were you doing, anyway?' he asked. 'Having a treasure hunt?'

She had decided she would keep the truth from everyone but Paul and Maria, who knew most of it already. 'Just exploring,' she told him.

'Well, you should at least call on me,' he said. 'I'm always happy to escort you wherever you want to go, and I can point out a few of the booby traps.'

She thought his choice of words oddly appropriate. She had indeed walked into a booby trap, but surely only one other person would have known that.

Ray left when Paul returned. Paul dismissed Maria, who went shuffling back to her kitchen. But when he came to stand by Jeannie's bed, he looked more concerned than ever.

'Well,' she asked him, 'Did you find any clues to who was lurking in the attic?'

He shook his head. 'No one was in the attic,' he said.

'But that's not possible!' she exclaimed. 'Of course someone was there. I saw the light behind the door.'

He shook his head again. 'No,' he repeated, 'I took a ladder and went up. That room hasn't been disturbed for years, probably a decade or more. Not even a mouse could move up there without leaving an obvious trail.'

'Then . . . maybe someone outside . . . ' she offered lamely.

'There's just one broken window, with no ledges outside, and no stairs. It faces onto the courtyard and it's three long stories down to the ground. There's simply no way anyone could have been in that room.'

'But, Paul, I saw the light. It was

moving around.' He made no reply and after a minute, she sighed and said, 'I just don't understand.'

He helped her to get out of bed and she found that except for a little stiffness she could manage to get around quite well. Maria came back with some hot soup and some chocolate for her. Paul remained with her.

She had been turning a thought around in her mind while she ate and when she had finished and put the tray aside, she shared it with him. 'I think I ought to leave here,' she said.

He was taken aback. 'But why?'

'What happened tonight ought to be reason enough,' she said. 'I don't know how it was done, but I don't believe in ghosts, either. Someone wanted me hurt, maybe even dead.'

He managed a smile but not a very happy one. 'So you can be frightened after all. I was beginning to think you had no fear in you.'

She laughed at that but she grew quickly sober. 'No, it isn't really that, although that can't be entirely ignored either.' She groped for the right words. 'There are mysteries here, things that you can't or won't explain to me. If I remain, they will always be a wall between us. I'm willing to trust you, truly; willing to believe that the blame does not lie with you, but I couldn't live here and just put all that out of my mind.'

'I can't let you leave,' he said firmly. 'I won't let you leave.'

'Then can you tell me everything?' she asked bluntly. 'All the details of your wife's death, all the secrets you've so far kept from me?'

He covered his face with his hands. 'No,' he said finally. 'I can't. Not yet.'

'Then I've got to go,' she said.

'I love you.' It was a cry of anguish. 'And you love me. Isn't that enough?'

They both knew that what he said was true. But she knew as well that it wasn't enough. 'The other would destroy us,' she said.

After a moment he stood, in control of himself again. 'Give me one day more,' he asked. 'Tomorrow it will all be over, I promise you.'

She thought of something then that had puzzled her in the past. 'Paul, why have none of the girls who worked here ever left the island?'

'I don't know what you mean,' he said, looking puzzled. 'They all left. Oh, there was a coincidence of tragedies. One girl ran away from home, and another was drowned in a boating accident.' He smiled tolerantly. 'You've been listening to village gossip.'

'Yes. But everyone there seems so certain that no one ever comes back from here. There were two other girls also and neither of them ever came back to the town.'

'But of course they did,' he said. 'They had to. They left here and that's the nearest landing.'

She shook her head stubbornly. 'The people in Grandy's Landing seem quite positive they did not return.'

For a moment he said and did nothing. His face darkened and she knew he was weighing what she had told him against what he himself knew.

'None of them?' he asked finally.

'Not a one,' she replied.

'Then I've been the worst kind of fool,' he said shortly. He turned and went swiftly from the room, his face an angry mask.

18

She waited anxiously for Paul to return. When an hour had passed and still there was no sign of him, she donned a robe and stole down the dark hall to his room. He was not there either.

She went back to her own room and dressed hurriedly. The house seemed ominously still as she came downstairs. She saw no one except for Maria, still at work in the kitchen although it was already late. She looked surprised to see Jeannie.

'Have you seen Mr. Langdon — Paul, that is?' Jeannie asked her. Maria shook her head no.

He was not in his study either, but as she stood just inside that doorway she had a glimpse of a light moving rapidly across the courtyard. By the time she reached the shutters and opened them, it was gone.

Her coat was in the hall. She threw it

about her shoulders and hurried outside. The light had been moving toward the rear of the house, where the gate opened onto the paths that led to the rest of the island. She went in the same direction. Her first impulse was to follow that path that she and Ray and Varda had taken previously, the one that led to the beach; but as she hesitated at the gate, she again saw the elusive light.

Just like in the attic, she told herself angrily.

This time someone was moving with a lamp across the crumbling spine of land that joined the house with the separate building that had formerly been the servants' quarters. At this distance she could not see who was carrying the lamp, but as she watched, it disappeared inside that structure.

She went after it, picking her way carefully over stones and crumbling earth. The old building and the piece of land on which it sat were like a finger pointing out into the ocean. The ridge was only a few feet wide and on either side she could look down at the roaring ocean. In places the path had been completely obliterated and she had almost to crawl over debris.

She had not taken time to question the motive that drove her along this dangerous trail. She knew that if she encountered anyone hostile here she would be hard pressed to avoid tragedy, but instinct told her she was near the end of the maze she had been travelling. She felt compelled to learn who was in that building that Ray had told her was never used, and why they were there at this late hour. And she felt certain, without understanding how it was possible, that whoever was responsible for the light that had led her here had been responsible as well for the light in the attic.

She stopped suddenly as a beam of light warned her of an approach. Someone stepped from the building in front of her. He lifted the lamp to check his footing and she let out her breath in a grateful sigh.

'Paul,' she called softly, hurrying toward him. She stumbled just before she reached him and he sprang forward to put an arm about her, but he looked anything but glad to see her.

'Why are you here?' he asked.

'I followed you,' she said breathlessly, glad for the feel of his strong arm about her. She was more bruised and stiff than she had realized before. 'Or, rather, I followed your light. Paul, what is it?'

Some great shock had lined his face deeply. She glanced past him, at the crumbling structure from which he had just emerged.

'What did you find?' she asked.

'I haven't been in there in six or seven years,' he said in a strained voice, holding her close, 'but I am certain that when I last looked inside, there were no graves in the dirt floor.'

She gasped in astonishment. 'Oh, Paul, no.'

He pulled her gently away from the door, to a broken pile of rocks where they could sit and look down on the ocean. She sat secure in the curve of his arm.

'I wanted to wait until tomorrow to explain to you,' he said, 'because by then I planned to have Varda away from here. I thought it would be best if you did not

246

know until she was gone.'

'Varda? What has she got to do with graves in that old building?'

'Varda is marked with the Langdon curse,' he said grimly.

'Oh, darling, I can't believe that,' she cried, clinging more tightly to him. 'Surely you can't believe it either, all those old ghost stories?'

'Do you think I wanted to believe it?' he asked, his voice thick with grief. 'Before my father died, in one of his saner moments, he warned me against having children. He was convinced that the curse would mark them. From the moment Varda was born, I've lived in dread of seeing his prophecy fulfilled.'

He sat in silence for several minutes. She waited patiently for him to continue.

'The night my wife died, I was away. She was in her room — the same room you're occupying now. She was taking drugs, sleeping pills, and everyone thought she was in bed for the night. Suddenly she began screaming, so loudly she could be heard throughout the house. Maria was the first to reach her room, but it took several minutes to get there from the kitchen, and it was too late. Susan had already fallen from the balcony, but there was blood all about the room, especially on her bed.'

'Someone had attacked her?'

'That's how it appeared. It looked as though she had been attacked in her sleep, had awakened in terror and fled to the balcony in panic or shock, to fall to her death.'

Jeannie closed her eyes, thinking of those windows opening over the rocks and the ocean. Beneath her the waves pounded and she almost thought she could hear Susan's terrified screaming over the roar of the ocean.

'Maria's first thought was for Varda,' he went on. 'She's completely devoted to the child, as you must have realized. She went to Varda's room. What she saw there made her lock the room up and wait for me in the courtyard. When I came home, an hour or so later, she took me straight to Varda's room. My daughter was asleep, but her face and her nightclothes were smeared with blood.' Jeannie gasped.

'When Susan's body was found, there was a wound on her throat. Of course I had to tell my brother and mother what I had seen. We questioned Varda, as gently as we could, but she remembered nothing. She seemed to have blocked everything from her mind.'

'Good heavens,' Jeannie murmured, her head spinning with the impact of his story.

'Since then,' he said, 'I've lived with the full horror of the knowledge that my daughter has inherited the family curse. I've done everything I could to prevent further harm. That's why I sleep in her room with the door locked. She can't harm anyone but me that way, but she doesn't have to be alone either. I wouldn't have let you come here if I'd known in advance, but my mother made those arrangements, and when I questioned them, she argued that Varda had to be given some education unless she is to remain an animal all her life.'

He paused again and sighed. 'But that was foolishness, of course. I was only avoiding what I knew I would have to do.

There's a hospital not far away on the mainland. My father stayed there during some of his worst spells. I've arranged for Varda to go there. I meant to take her across early in the morning. There's a rental car waiting for me in town. I planned to be back here by noon, when I would tell you all of this.'

'Must you . . . take her there?' she asked.

'Yes, it's best. And it's a good place, I know. She'll be educated and cared for and perhaps helped.'

She knew he was right. It was the only sensible course of action, but her heart ached for the girl. 'It's so hard for me to believe,' she said.

'I wish that were all of it,' he said in a low voice.

She looked up into his face. The moonlight made his silver eyes gleam eerily. 'What more could there be?' she asked.

'Varda couldn't have done that,' he said, motioning toward the abandoned building.

She brought a hand to her throat. She

had forgotten his grim discovery. 'But then . . . ?'

'That's a man's work.'

'Do you think Franz . . . ?'

'That's too cunning for him. Franz thinks like a brute. He'd have thrown them into the ocean. No, it has to be the curse, and it has to be a Langdon. That could only mean Ray.'

They sat in silence for a moment. She was too stunned to know what to say or do. Finally he stood, helping her to her feet. 'Here,' he said, handing her the lamp. 'You go on back. Tell Maria to wake my mother. I'll have to tell her about this.'

'What about you?' she asked.

He smiled gently at the concern in her eyes. 'I'll be along in a few minutes,' he said. 'I have to be entirely certain that those graves in there really are graves. I don't see what else they could be, but I don't want to jump to unwarranted conclusions.' He turned her around firmly. 'Go along. And watch your step.'

She did not argue with his desire to be alone with his grisly work. She knew what a shock this discovery must be to him;

and not only did he need to confirm what he'd found, but he also must have time to sort out his thoughts and to reach some decisions. She must grow accustomed to the fact that he would not always need her, at least not in the most direct and obvious ways.

She went back faster than she had come. Once she looked back over her shoulder, but the dark shadows hid Paul and she might only have dreamed the entire scene.

She was almost to the house when she met Ray. He came so quickly and so unexpectedly out of the darkness that he had taken hold of her wrist before she even knew he was there. She gasped and dropped the lamp. It shattered, the oil flaming for a moment, and then going out.

'What are you doing out here?' he asked in a tense whisper.

'I was . . . ' But she was too frightened to think of a plausible excuse.

He glanced once past her, at the abandoned house, and then looked hard into her face. 'So you've found what's out there?'

The shock of what Paul had just told her left her with too little emotional reserve. She was seized suddenly with a fear too great to be contained. With a whimpering cry she wrenched free of his grip and darted past him, but she had taken only a few steps before she stumbled on a loose rock and fell to the ground.

19

'Ray.' It was Paul's voice. Jeannie scrambled to her knees in time to see Paul charge down upon his brother.

Ray had time only to cry, 'Don't!' His protest was futile in the face of Paul's rage.

Ray was no match for his brother. The fight was over in a minute, Ray unconscious on the ground. Paul helped Jeannie to her feet. 'Are you all right?' he asked anxiously.

She gave him a shaky nod. 'Yes, thanks to you.'

'I saw the lamp fall and thought you had stumbled. I didn't see Ray until I was almost here.'

They both looked down at the unconscious man on the ground. 'I'm going tonight,' Paul said. 'I'm taking both of them, Ray and Varda, to the hospital. That's the best thing I can do for them as well as for us.' He turned his attention to her. 'Go get Varda, dress her warmly, and bring her down to the boat landing. And have Maria wake my mother. Tell her to come down to the landing too. I'll have to explain to her.'

Without waiting to see if she followed his instructions, he bent and lifted his brother effortlessly, throwing him over his shoulder.

★ ★ ★

Maria was still working in the kitchen. She hurried off at once to do Jeannie's bidding. Varda was asleep when Jeannie let herself into her room. At first she was uncomprehending, but then she got excited at the idea of a night excursion with her father. Jeannie's heart felt as though it were breaking within her and she had to fight to hold back the tears.

'You're going to a new home,' she explained in answer to Varda's breathless questions.

'Will I stay there forever?'

Jeannie helped her into a warm coat. 'Not forever, but for a while. And it's a bright sunny place, not dark and gloomy like this one.'

Varda's face clouded over. 'Aren't you going to live there with me?'

Jeannie gave her a quick hug. 'No, but I promise that I'll come often to visit with you, and so will your daddy and your grandmother. And you'll have a lot of new friends.'

Beatrice was at the landing when Jeannie and Varda arrived. From the older woman's pained expression, Jeannie knew Paul had already told her what he meant to do. She looked on the verge of tears, but she managed to smile bravely as she embraced Varda.

Ray was still unconscious, lying in the launch. Paul had tied his hands with a piece of rope in case he woke up during the trip. Jeannie waited for an opportune moment when the others weren't looking and handed Paul the gun from her room. He said nothing but slipped it into his pocket.

'Why is Uncle Ray tied up?' Varda asked when she had been handed into the boat.

'I'll explain that to you on the way,' her

father promised. 'But you'll have to sit with me like a grown-up girl.'

'I am a grown-up girl,' she said firmly.

Paul leaned out of the boat to embrace Jeannie briefly. 'I'm afraid it will be close to dawn before I get back,' he said.

'I'll wait for you in my room,' she promised.

She watched until the launch's running lights had disappeared into the darkness. Beatrice did not, however. She turned and went slowly up the steps as soon as Paul had pulled away from the landing. Despite her regal bearing and her strong self-control, she looked weary and beaten down just now. Jeannie could only imagine what she must be feeling. She had lost a husband to this strange curse, and now she was losing a son and a granddaughter.

The water lay high on the rocks of the landing. The tide was coming in. It would soon be high tide. By the time those waters had receded, Jeannie told herself, Paul would have come back to her. With that thought warm inside her, she followed Beatrice up the rocky steps.

She built up the fire in her room and did not change into her nightgown but left her dress on. She brought a blanket from the bed and wrapping it around her legs, curled up in the big chair before the fire.

It had been a long and eventful evening and she was quite tired, but she knew she would not sleep until Paul had returned. She knew, too, that having carried out his painful errand, he would need the renewing strength of her love.

It was nearly an hour later when Beatrice knocked softly and came in, bearing a silver tray, with a small pot and two cups. 'I saw your light,' she said, 'and thought perhaps you would drink a cup of chocolate with me. I can't sleep either.'

'Thank you, that's very thoughtful of you.' Jeannie brought a second chair over by the fireplace.

'Shall I bring my sewing and sit with you for a while?' Beatrice asked. There was something so plaintive in her tone that Jeannie could hardly refuse, although in fact she would have preferred to be alone.

'Of course,' she said. 'We'll wait for Paul together.'

She realized, while Beatrice was gone, that the chocolate was making her sleepy. She carefully poured the rest of her cup back into the pot so that it would appear she had finished it. Even the few sips she had taken made her feel incredibly drowsy. She was on the verge of dozing off when Beatrice returned with her embroidery basket.

'Go ahead and sleep,' Beatrice said, taking her chair and spreading a piece of embroidery across her lap. 'I'll watch for my son.'

Jeannie shook her head, trying to dispel the drifting sensation that was plaguing her. 'No, I'll be all right in a minute,' she said. 'Perhaps if you opened the windows and let some fresh air in.'

'Of course.' Beatrice set her embroidery aside and went to open the windows. The night wind brought with it the tangy scent of the ocean. It revived Jeannie somewhat, but it was cold, too, and she had to wrap the blanket around herself.

Beatrice had remained standing at the

window, a curtain blowing across one shoulder. She stared out at the night. 'Your sister fell from this very window,' she said in a near monotone, without turning. 'I watched her from right next to her bed.'

Jeannie's eyes snapped open. A warning bell had sounded somewhere far back in her mind but she could not seem to pull her thoughts together. They kept drifting . . . to and fro, in and out . . . drifting . . . drifting . . .

' . . . hated her so,' Beatrice said in a voice dripping venom. 'Making us beg for her blasted money. I pleaded with her that very night. I told her how drastic the situation was. She only laughed at me. Yes, she actually laughed.'

The chocolate, Jeannie thought. It had tasted a bit strange, with a bitter after-taste. Before, she had been wide awake. It was after she sipped the chocolate that she became so drowsy. *But I drank so little*, one part of her mind told her. *If I fight it I can stay awake. I have only to resist it with all my energy.*

' . . . said the only way we'd get any

more of her money was over her dead body . . . '

The clouds parted for a moment. 'You called her my sister,' she said aloud. Her tongue felt swollen and fuzzy. 'You know about that?'

Beatrice laughed — a high, shrill laugh. 'Do you think I'm a fool? I've known almost from the beginning. Ray asked around in town, and learned who you were, and he told me. It only amused him. Nearly everything amuses Ray. He's a fool. As you were, to come here.'

The dizziness was coming and going in waves, leaving her a little clearer-headed with each receding wave, a little more nearly asleep as each broke over her. She struggled to sit upright, finally managing to focus her eyes on Beatrice. The woman's face was a mask of evil malice.

'You killed Susan,' Jeannie said.

Beatrice laughed again, her eyes flashing. 'No, I didn't kill the little ninny, although I meant to. I came back to try one more time to make her understand, and she was asleep. She had knocked herself silly with those pills of hers — the same pills you had in your chocolate. And that's when I knew that her time had come. I took the scissors from my sewing basket . . . '

Jeannie's eyes dropped to the scissors, right in front of her.

'Yes, those very same scissors . . . but the fool woke up and began screaming when she saw blood. She staggered out of bed only half-conscious, and ran straight for the windows. I watched her plunge through, and fall to her death.'

'But, Varda?' Jeannie mumbled. It was coming again, that awful darkness, sickeningly oppressive, threatening this time to carry her away. She gasped for breath, feeling smothered, trying to throw off the blanket. The cold wind would revive her, if she could get free of the blanket.

'I went to her room. I thought the screams would have frightened her, but she was still asleep. I kissed her and then I went away and cleaned myself up.'

It was so foolish to struggle, really; so much nicer to let herself float gently upward on a soft, fluffy cloud — drifting, not caring, blessedly at peace. It was pink, this cloud of hers, like long-forgotten cotton candy, and it swayed and rocked comfortingly back and forth.

Her eyes fluttered open again. She struggled to remain awake, but the darkness was so overwhelming.

'Franz will take care of you for me, as he has all the others. And I'll tell Paul that you ran away, that you really loved Ray and you did not want to stay here without him. Women are always falling in love with Ray. Every one of those foolish girls did . . . and when you're gone, why, we'll be happy here again, just the Langdons . . . ' Her voice sounded closer. It droned on an on, with almost no inflection now. 'Yes, sleep, that's a good girl. Sleep now. Beatrice will stay with you until you're sound asleep.'

Jeannie's eyes opened one more time, then closed and remained closed. She sank back into the softness of the chair and a deep sigh escaped her lips.

She was still.

20

As though from far, far away, she heard the door close. *Now,* she told herself firmly. *Now I will open my eyes and I will be wide awake. Now!*

She did, finally, manage to open her eyes, but she saw the room as though through water. She could not quite bring herself to full wakefulness; could not make her feet push against the floor to get her out of the chair. The little table with the silver tray and the pot of chocolate stood nearby. She reached for the table and missed. She reached again and this time managed to close her fingers upon the edge of the tray. She tugged and it came spilling across the chair and across her, the still-hot liquid splashing from the pot to burn her arm and wrist.

It was the shock she needed. She woke with a violent jerk of her head. Now she could rise from the chair, swaying unsteadily. She thought of the gun Lou had given her, and immediately remembered that she had given the gun to Paul — and Paul would be gone for hours.

Her sense of time was distorted and she could not think clearly. How long had Beatrice been gone? Seconds? Minutes? An hour?

She began to slap her face hard, first one cheek and then the other. The stinging blows helped. She stumbled to the window, clutching at the open panes to keep her balance, and gulped in deep breaths of air. Gradually she began to regain possession of her faculties.

She would have to escape. If she could reach a boat, she could get to the village and wait for Paul there. If not, she would have to find someplace to hide until he came back. There was no question in her mind that between now and then, Beatrice intended to kill her.

At least now she was able to walk steadily. The drug must have been very potent that so little of it should have had such a strong effect, but she'd had experience with Susan and her sleeping pills, and she knew that those sleeping drugs which take the most immediate and powerful effect also wear off the fastest. If she could keep herself moving for a while, she would soon be herself again.

She dared not take a lamp. The shadows that had seemed her enemies in the past were now her only allies in this house. She paused in the hall, thinking of Maria. Paul trusted her. Dared she go to Maria for help?

But even if Maria wanted to help her, would she stand up both to her husband and to the matriarch of the Langdon clan? No, she couldn't risk turning to Maria. Until Paul returned in the morning, she was completely on her own.

She had almost reached the front door, moving more rapidly now as the effects of the drug began to wear off, when Beatrice herself stepped from the parlor directly into Jeannie's path.

'Stop,' she cried, putting up her hands as if to catch Jeannie.

Jeannie ran, literally knocking Beatrice aside. Attracted by the cry, Maria stepped out of the kitchen, but Jeannie was past her before the maid could attempt to stop her. Another few seconds and she was at the door, bursting through, outside. If she could just get to one of the boats . . .

She was almost to the gate that led to the landing when Franz stepped through it, coming toward the house. They both stopped short, staring in surprise.

'Franz, stop her!' Beatrice shrieked from the doorway.

Jeannie turned and ran in the opposite direction, across the courtyard. She heard Maria cry, 'Franz, no,' and sounds of a scuffle. She looked once over her shoulder in time to see Franz throw his wife to the ground and start after her.

She had a head start on him, however, and Franz was slow and clumsy. She was out of the courtyard almost before he had started to run.

Three paths. One led to the abandoned outbuilding where Paul had discovered the graves. That was a dead end. The second led downhill, into the island wilderness where she knew wild pigs and other animals ran free.

She chose the path that led perilously down the side of the cliff, to the beach.

Maybe she could find a place to hide there, among the rocks.

But this path was not to her advantage. It was too narrow and dangerous for her to do more than crawl along, and Franz, who knew it better than she did, could move with more confidence.

She could hear his deep breathing behind her, seeming closer and closer. As she neared the bottom, she began to run. The ground gave beneath her and she went sliding and tumbling the last few feet.

She was on her feet again at once, kicking off her slippers to run barefoot across the wet sand. Ahead of her was the wall of rock that held in the little private beach. The strip of sand she was on grew narrower. The wet sand was now covered with water that was deeper and deeper as she approached the rocks.

She stopped suddenly, horrified. The tide was coming in, cutting off escape from this little cove. Ray had warned her how the rocks held it back until it was nearly full tide. Then, as the water cleared the wall of rock, it rushed over the secluded beach like a tidal wave.

She looked back. Franz had thought of the same thing apparently, for he too had stopped. Seeing her motionless, however, he began to run again.

She had no choice now but to go on. If she could cross that patch of sand and reach the cliffs, she might find some sanctuary, some spot where she could climb above the waterline and wait out the tide. It was her only hope.

She banged her leg on a sharp rock hidden beneath the water's surface. She was almost hip-deep in the water now, fighting against the rushing tide. She got a handhold on the rock and climbed upward, scrambling over the cold, wet stone.

Franz was there in a moment, reaching for her. His outstretched hand grazed her leg and caught her skirt. She threw herself forward, to the sand on the other side, the fabric ripping in his grasp.

Her lungs were bursting. She felt as if she had no strength left in her limbs. How wonderful it would be just to lie where she was, to let the water wash over her . . .

The water *was* washing over her! It

brought her back to reality and she scrambled up again just as Franz landed beside her. She stumbled a few feet more before her legs gave out on her and she fell again. Gasping for breath, she looked toward her pursuer, knowing that the race was his.

He was not looking at her now, though. He had turned to stare in horror at the water rushing over the rocks. The false tide was swamping the beach. A torrent swept over her, lifting her from the sand and carrying her along with it. It rolled back briefly, giving her a moment to spit sea water from her mouth and gasp for air, and then she was struggling against a rushing flood of water that sent her rolling and tumbling over and over until she had been slammed against a boulder.

She tried to swim but the current was too violent. The pressure holding her against the boulder shifted, then grabbed her again and she was being dragged, as if by giant hands, further along the beach. There was no air to breathe now; her choking efforts only filled her lungs with water.

As though in a dream she heard Paul calling her name. 'Jeannie!' he shouted from far away. 'Jeannie!'

Her head was above water. She crashed against another boulder, a huge one. She clung to it, trying to climb up.

'Jeannie!'

This was no dream. It was Paul, calling her name.

'Paul!' she screamed, redoubling her efforts to climb upward. A brilliant beam of light shot past her, a short distance in front of her, then arced back. Suddenly it was full upon her, seeming to give her the strength to cling where she was.

'Hold on,' he shouted.

But she couldn't hold on; her hands were too weak. 'Hurry,' she called back, her grip beginning to loosen. The rock was cutting into her hands; the water tugged at her, wanting her back in its grip. She felt herself slipping but hadn't the breath left to call for Paul again.

Then he was there, his strong arm about her. They were in the water but he had a rope around them and was dragging them toward the boat. She held on to him with her remaining strength, wishing she could help and knowing that it wasn't necessary, that he would do it all.

She had a dim impression of Ray in the boat, helping to pull them in, and Varda's wide eyes as she was lifted limply into the launch. After that there was only darkness and, at last, the sleep that had been waiting to claim her.

★ ★ ★

Jeannie felt awful. There wasn't an inch of her that didn't ache. She did not want to wake up and tried to crawl back into the blanket of sleep, but now it eluded her and somewhere nearby she heard voices.

She opened her eyes finally. She was in her room, in bed. Ray and Paul were talking nearby.

'She's finally asleep,' Ray was saying. 'Maria's with her. And Varda's asleep in her own bed. Hello, look who's awake though.' They both turned toward her.

She managed a very weak smile. Paul came to the bed and took her hand. 'It's all right,' he said softly. 'I'm here now. No one will hurt you, not ever again.'

'Your mother . . . ' she tried to say, but her voice failed her.

'I know,' he said. 'She'll be taken into custody, and will have to stand trial for her crimes . . . ' He paused, and went on bitterly, 'When I think what I did to poor little innocent Varda . . . '

'When did you learn the truth?' Jeannie asked.

'When Ray came to in the boat, he told me what I had done. He had just made the same discovery in the old building that I had, and was on his way to tell me about it. He'd even figured out your ghostly lights.'

'Mother's bedroom is directly across the courtyard from that old attic,' Ray said when she looked at him. 'All she had to do was sit at her window and shine a flashlight across. From outside the room it looked like someone moving around in there with a lamp.'

'We got back as fast as we could,' Paul said, 'but it almost wasn't fast enough. We saw you run across the cliff, with Franz after you, or we'd have gone directly to the landing, and we'd have been too late.'

She smiled at him, too lethargic to want to say much, but a thought came to her all at once. 'You called me Jeannie,' she said. 'Back there, in the water. But . . . you knew . . . ?'

'Didn't you know how Susan idolized you?' he asked. 'She carried your picture everywhere she went.'

'Then you knew all along, from the very first?' He nodded, grinning. 'But why did you pretend not to know? Why didn't you send me away that first day?'

'Didn't the last place you lived have any mirrors either?' he asked. 'Between falling in love at first sight, and being angry that you had come under a false name, I didn't know whether to kiss you or throw you back into the ocean.'

Notwithstanding the delay, he seemed finally to have made a choice. She thought when his kiss was ended that he had more than made up for any delays.

'Do I get a turn?' Ray asked.

'Not unless you want a sock in the jaw,' Paul told him without looking around.

Ray rubbed a badly bruised spot on his chin. 'Thanks, but one of those a night is enough for me.'

After a short while, since there was no more conversation, he left them. They were only vaguely aware of his going.

THE END

TERROR STRIKES

Norman Firth

To Chief Inspector Sharkey, the first murder is baffling enough: on a nightclub dance floor, a man suddenly begins to choke. Horrified onlookers watch as he collapses and dies. It is quickly established that he has been strangled by someone standing directly behind him. But witnesses all testify that there was no one near him to do it. When this death is followed by a whole string of similar murders, Sharkey begins to seriously wonder if Scotland Yard is up against something supernatural . . .

THE JOCKEY

Gerald Verner

A man calling himself the Jockey begins a campaign against those who he believes have besmirched the good name of horse racing, escaping conviction through lack of evidence. In a message to the press, he vows that those who have amassed crooked fortunes will have the money taken from them, whilst those who have caused loss of life will find their own lives forfeit . . . When the murders begin, Superintendent Budd of Scotland Yard is charged to find and stop the mysterious avenger. But is the Jockey the actual murderer?

MURDER AT ST. MARK'S

Norman Firth

Dr. Wignall, Headmaster of the venerable public school of St. Mark's, is fiercely proud of the institution. But this pride has been considerably shaken by the murder of a teacher's daughter in the nearby woods. As Mr. Prenderby, the charismatic master of North House, uncovers a sordid undercurrent of gambling, blackmail and immorality amongst the schoolboys, another murder is committed — this time, one of the pupils. When one of the teachers bolts, the police think they are trailing the killer — but are they?

THE BISHOP'S PALACE

V. J. Banis

Elizabeth Parker comes to Brazil to take up a job as a schoolteacher in the declining city of Manalos, skirting the Amazonian jungle. Hoping to start a new life, she instead finds forbidden love with the husband of her employer, the aristocratic Kitty Drayton, who lives in a decaying mansion with her spinster sister. The atmosphere of unease surrounding Elizabeth steadily grows into terror as she is stalked by a sinister figure during Rio's Carnival, culminating in a shocking murder — for which she becomes the obvious suspect . . .

THE SILVER HORSESHOE

Gerald Verner

John Arbinger receives an anonymous note — offering 'protection' from criminal gangs in exchange for £5,000 — with the impression of a tiny silver horseshoe in the bottom right-hand corner. Ignoring the author's warning about going to the police, Arbinger seeks the help of Superintendent Budd of Scotland Yard. But Budd is too late to save Arbinger from the deadly consequences of his actions, and soon the activities of the Silver Horseshoe threaten the public at large — as well as the lives of Budd and his stalwart companions . . .

A MURDER MOST MACABRE

Edmund Glasby

Jeremy Lavelle, leader of the esoteric Egyptian Society the Order of the True Sphinx, has illegally purchased an ancient Egyptian mummy. Watched by his enthralled followers, he opens the coffin and begins to unwrap the body . . . The head is that of an ancient scribe, his shrivelled and desiccated face staring eyelessly up from his coffin — yet from the neck down, wrapped up in layers of bandages, are not the mummified remains which they had expected. Instead, they stare in horror at the decapitated corpse of a recently killed man!